MOTHER/DAUGHTER MONOLOGUES

From the International Centre for Women Playwrights

Volume 1:

Babes and Beginnings

ISBN: 978-0-557-09422-6

Original Cover Photo:

© Tami Bone, 2009, used with permission.

http://www.tamibonephotographs.com

PUBLISHED BY THE **ICWP PRESS**, COLUMBUS, OHIO, UNITED STATES OF AMERICA, 2009.

FOREWORD

Writing a monologue is the first assignment I give beginning students in dramatic writing. Writing a successful monologue is not an easy assignment for any writer. A successful monologue is a tiny play: it must have a defined story with a beginning, middle, and end, it must have conflict, demonstrating an active choice presented to and taken by the speaker, and it must lead to a resolution, a conclusion of that conflict and choice. A good monologue reveals an interesting character in action interacting with two audiences, the one onstage, to whom the character speaks directly, and the one in the auditorium, who observes.

The monologue is not the equivalent of a soliloquy; in the latter, the character is alone on stage and thus speaks only to herself, or to a cosmic force, or to the audience. She is moved, in great part, by her loneliness in that performance space, looking inside or beyond its boundaries to make contact.

But when a character speaks in a monologue, she reaches out to other characters onstage, revealing, cajoling, seducing, bargaining, attacking, driving her words at and into the beings surrounding her. Their silence—which must exist in order for her to monologue—spurs her to choice and to action and, finally, to transformation.

The transformation of the speaker, her onstage listeners, and the audience in their seats.

Choosing a monologue for auditions is a difficult process, especially for young actors. While some beautiful monologues for young women exist in the classical canon—Juliet, Viola, and Nina among the few—there are not enough, and certainly not enough effective ones, and far too few contemporary choices. And by "effective" I mean age-appropriate, intelligent, and theatrical. Monologues that allow young actresses to demonstrate and stretch their muscles (vocal and physical) as well as their imagination. Monologues that empower them, young as they are, rather than strip them of self-respect by suggesting that a "good" monologue performance requires blue language, mature sexuality, and highlighting physical "assets."

Fortunately, this collection of monologues, written by contemporary women playwrights (*and some male supporters - ed.*), offers young actresses moving and effective material while, simultaneously, focusing it on characters and conflicts close to home. These young female characters, ranging in age from their teens to late 20s, face crises of faith, of family, of loss, of happiness, often from the vantage point of youth, discovery, and initiation. The writers give their characters pain, courage, fear, humor, and joy.

And, rather delightfully, all the proceeds of this work and its sister volumes will be recycled back into development money for women playwrights, supporting the ongoing production and publication of women's dramatic writing across the globe. I am proud to be part of such fierce support for the work of my fellow writers and for young actresses everywhere.

—Dr. Gretchen Elizabeth Smith

Head of Theatre Studies, Division of Theatre

Southern Methodist University, Dallas, Texas, USA

علم

TABLE OF CONTENTS

From "JUICE"

By Patricia Montley, USA

A GIRL DAUGHTER, 11-13

Productions: The Women's Project at Theatre Project, Baltimore, March, 1996
Love Creek Short Play Festival, Harold Clurman Theatre, NYC, July, 1996
Slightly Askew Players, Santa Barbara, CA, 1997
Echo Theatre, Dallas, TX, 1999 (reading)
Conference of the Society for Menstrual Cycle Research, Pittsburgh, 2003

GIRL (DAUGHTER): The thing is, I feel out of control. It's like I've been invaded by the body snatchers or something. For a while now my body's been...well, out of control. I don't know how to explain it. But I think I'm...not normal. I've got too much...*juice.* I mean when I go to the dentist to get a tooth filled and he jams all those little cotton logs in my mouth, well they get soggy real fast. And if he forgets to put that thing in—that suction hook—well, in no time at all, I'm like drooling uncontrollably. The juice is running down my chin and onto the stupid bib. And if I think about it—try to stop it with, you know, mind over matter—it only gets worse. I tell you, I'm out of control.

It's like my body has a life of its own. It does things it never used to do before—things I don't tell it to do. Like sweat. Major sweat. I don't mean a little dampness at the hair line after shooting baskets. I could handle that. I'm talking great rivers of body odor sweat pouring out my armpits...making gigantic ugly half moons on my blouse so I can't comb my hair or wave my arm without grossing out everybody in the room. I mean what's the point anyway? Why does it have to do that? And for no good reason. I mean sometimes I'm not even doing anything physical. I don't mind it in the gym. You expect it there. Hey—you take a towel. But this other stuff—it's weird. Like last month I was riding my bicycle out in the country and I went through this tunnel—you know, a covered bridge. It wasn't a long tunnel or anything. Just a regular size tunnel. Anyway, all the sudden I felt kinda sick—what my grandmother calls woozy. I felt kinda woozy and then whisshhh! I was wet all over. My hands were sweating all over the stupid handlebars. My glasses were sliding down my nose. When I got through the tunnel, it went away just like that—the sick feeling. Of course, the sweat took a little longer. And now I've started to have this regular dream—I'm running down this tunnel—a long one this time. I'm running hard and fast and I'm sweating and sweating, and the water's rolling off me onto the ground, and soon the water's up to my knees and then my waist and then my neck and I have to swim out, only I can't see where "out" is because now my eyes are under water too, and I can't get above water level because the water's right up to the top of the tunnel, and I swim and I swim...and then suddenly I wake up and I'm face down on the bed and I'm soaked in sweat. *(Beat.)* Like I said, it's weird.

And the other thing that's even more embarrassing, of course...is, well, you know, I never know when *"it's"* going to strike. So I can't plan things. I mean, who wants to go camping with cramps? And what if you're out on the dance floor, in like white jeans or something, and all the guys are leaning against the wall behind you. Or like one night I slept over at Peggy Burkehart's; and they have a big family so they eat all their meals—even breakfast—in the dining room. And they just had this new upholstery put on the chairs—it was pale blue. And right in the middle of eating hot cakes, I felt this swooping feeling in my gut and then I just lifted myself an inch off the chair 'cause I just knew there'd be a stain. And I sort of backed out of the room. God it was awful. Peggy came up to the bathroom and called in to tell me where the tampons were. Her mother acted like nothing had happened, like she didn't even notice my body had been taken over by some...lunar alien!

So, OK, I've got more saliva than I can comfortably swallow and I've got these unpredictable outbreaks of sweat, and once a month I'm seized by a lunar alien. But that's not the worst of it. No. The worst of it happens when I get these...these feelings. I mean the feelings aren't bad. The feelings are good. The feelings are wonderful. Sort of. Like when we went on the school picnic and I played tennis with Robert Russell who is in my algebra class and who I like a lot because he doesn't do dumb stuff like the other guys. And I beat him 6-2 and when we were walking back from the courts, he put his arm around me and said, "You're really good." And I was right up against his chest so close I could smell the fabric softener in his shirt. And right then, just at that minute, it happened. I got all wet...down there. I could feel it. A great gush of...I don't know...JUICE! *(Beat.)* But that's not all. Another time I was working in the library with Regina Callahan who has luscious auburn hair and who sings solos in the choir. And it was study hour so we weren't supposed to be talking. But she found this old yearbook and we were laughing together over some of the pictures because of the stupid hairdos, and she leaned over me to whisper something and the sun was making her hair all shimmery, and I could smell the cinnamon from the little red heart candies she was sucking on, and her mouth was so close to my ear I could feel how warm her breath was, and it made my ear all tingly and then, O my God, it happened again. *(Beat.)* I tell you, I'm out of control. It's scary. I don't know what I'm going to do.

THAT IS THAT

Adapted from "Suki Livingston Opens Like a Parachute"

By Robin Rice Lichtig, USA

SUKI is 12, unless she is older

SHE is repeating the story from memory. SHE speaks to the audience—or perhaps her grandmother.

SUKI: Mom about-faces, my head in tow like a football under her arm, and marches straight out of Chief of Police Royal's own office. On the ride home, she keeps her eyes on the road. She doesn't say one word. Does she think I did it? Mom? She's not gonna say. My eyes sting. My throat's tight. I won't cry. No sir. No sir. I push the gulp in my throat back down.

When we get home she takes off her coat, hangs it up, ties on an apron, starts washing the breakfast dishes. Her fingernail picks at a piece of dry egg on a plate like the egg is bad and she has to get rid of it before someone sees. The speck of egg flies off. She rinses it down the drain and dries her hands on her apron. That is that.

I'm a pond. Light sheers off and bounces back. Rain and wind, hail and snow don't affect me. You could ice skate on me and not leave a mark. You could drop an atom bomb and it wouldn't cause a ripple.

Wednesday after school I meet Alice at Hart's and order a banana split. Strawberry pink, pistachio green and chocolate ice cream. Butterscotch sauce. Confetti sprinkles. Three cherries. It looks like a circus. It tastes loud. I can't eat it. Alice figures it was the Turkel boys. I don't know. I don't know what the other kids think happened.

I start going to the art museum after school. Mostly I go by myself.

MOVING ON

By SuzAnne C. Cole, USA

ASHLEY, a pre-teen girl, blonde

SETTING: On stage right, a high stool where ASHLEY sits for her monologues. At stage left, a rug in front of a tall open box/cupboard with shelves. A sign on top of the box reads "The Art Room." The shelves hold art supplies and paper.)

TIME: the present

(AT RISE: Spotlight on ASHLEY who sits on the high stool. During her monologue she wanders around the stage, pulls paper from the "closet," etc.)

ASHLEY: I just don't like this house. Even if I do have my own room that Dad let me decorate all by myself. I wanted a room of my own 'cause sharing a room with Tracy was a pain. She's just a little kid. Still plays with dolls. And I'll be a teenager in a few years. But now...I wish Dad wasn't away so much. On business, he says.

I don't know why we had to move anyway. There wasn't anything wrong with our old house. Except sharing a room with Tracy. But Dad said Mother needed a change. She's been really strange. Ever since our baby brother was born. And then before he'd hardly been home at all, he was dead. Looked like he was just asleep...but he wasn't. Afterwards...I asked Mother if I could have my own room back since it didn't need to be a nursery anymore. But she started crying. And then she wouldn't talk to me. Not for days and days. Made me feel like a ghost.

There's this big closet at the end of the hall upstairs. When we moved in, Mother didn't put anything in it. Mother took art before our baby brother was born and died, but she doesn't paint or draw or anything any more. I asked her if we could have all her art stuff...if she wasn't gonna use it anymore. She didn't say no and she didn't say yes...she just stared at me like she does. So then I asked Dad if Tracy and me could use it and he said okay. The closet has these nice shelves. Tracy sits on the floor and uses the bottom shelf like a desk. I call the closet "The Art Room."

One day I go there looking for a big sheet of paper with no tears in it 'cause I have a picture in my head that wants to come out bad. And I find this spooky drawing. Two blonde-haired girls, maybe sisters, like us. Not playing though. Just lying down. Flat on the ground. The picture's not mine. And it looks way too good to be Tracy's, but I ask her anyway.

Sure enough, when I show it to her, she says, "Linda drew that."

"Linda?" I say. "A new friend?" Thinking good for her, 'cause I sure haven't made any friends here.

"No," she says. "She used to live here, her and Patty. Patty's her sister."

"How do you know?"

"She told me."

"You mean she still lives around here?"

"No. She talks to me in my head." Oh great. That's all this family needs right now. An invisible friend for Tracy.

"Have any more of her pictures?"

Tracy shows me a whole bunch more, way at the back of the closet. In a way, they're all the same picture. Two blonde girls, one bigger than the other one. Always sad. Eyes closed. Looking at them makes me feel all twisted up inside. I was gonna throw them away, but Tracy started crying, said Linda wouldn't like it.

A few days later, Tracy brings me another drawing with some writing on it and asks me to read it to her. This drawing is different. A woman standing outside a house. Looks like she's waving. Maybe waving good-bye to someone. The writing says, "This is a heartbreak house. Leave it while you can."

I'm angry and scared. I yell at Tracy, "Where'd you get this?" She says Linda left it in the art room. Just like the others. Then she wants to know what heartbreak means. I tell her it means sad. Sort of like Mother. I tell her I'll keep the picture for her and ask her to draw me a happy picture.

She says, "A family going to the circus?"

I tell her that'll be great. Then she says, "With a baby brother?"

I say, "No. . . . No baby. How about two sisters, one big, one little, just like us?

That was last month. More and more drawings of those same two girls, the ones who sorta look like Tracy and me, keep showing up in the art room. Now the girls are in boxes. Closed boxes. Underground. There are trees growing on top of them. I tried to get Mom to look once, but she just told me to leave her alone.

Tracy says she sees Linda and Patty waving good-bye. I don't think that closet's safe for Tracy. I'm going to take the art supplies and put them in my room. Tracy can come and draw with me.

I wish Dad would come home.

LIGHTS FADE TO BLACK

THE LETTER

By Maggie Gallant, British - USA

CATHERINE, 13 years old, tomboyish appearance

CATHERINE cracks open her bedroom door and listens. SHE closes it, obsessively touches the handle 3 times and sits down on her bed.

CATHERINE: She's read it, she must've read my letter, she's on the phone crying, probably to Aunt Laurie, telling her "my princess is gone," I hate it when she calls me princess. Thought she'd come and talk to me first. Hope my letter was ok.

"Dear Mum, please try not to be upset but there's something wrong with me and I have to tell you. Remember ages ago when we were at Camber Sands and I said I wanted to be a boy. What I meant is that I am a boy, on the inside. It's like I'm in the wrong body, an ugly girl body and I hate being Catherine. The real me is William, that's the name I've chosen, and I really want to be William for the rest of my life but I don't know how to. Please don't tell me I can't or say I'll grow out of this. I haven't told anybody else. I'll be in my room. Lots of love from, William (f.k.a. Catherine)."

I hope she could read my writing, she'll probably still correct my grammar. "No Catherine, you double the final consonant when adding a suffix."

At least I've finally told her, and before she finds out about my stupid period starting and wants to celebrate it. I don't know if getting my period means I can't ever be a boy. Wish I knew how to stop it, it's gross. What do I do if she won't let me be William?

I hope she comes in soon. I'm going to tell her everything. Like about crying when we did the nativity at school because they wouldn't let me be Joseph. And about shaving the heads of my Barbie dolls to make them into FBI agents not because I thought they had nits in their hair. And how I always sleep face down so my lumps won't grow bigger in the night.

Before these came at least I looked like a boy. When the checkout lady at Tesco's called me 'young man' by mistake it was the best thing that ever happened to me. Not to mum. Don't know who she was more cross at, then she has to remind me that my ugly body is a gift and starts humming All Things Bright and Beautiful.

She'll never admit that God messed up, that if he was so great he wouldn't make me like this. At least I don't waste time praying anymore, there's no point, I always wake up the same.

Wonder if she's off the phone yet.

(Cautiously opens bedroom door and looks out. Closes door, touches door handle three times, steps back)

She hasn't read my letter, it's still on the kitchen counter. She's got both TV's on, they're saying Princess Diana's died in a car crash, is that why she was crying?

(Sits silently and thinks)

Why today? Why did Di die today? Everything's ruined. I'll have to take the letter back, there's no point telling her now. And I'll have to get a new name, I can't be William, she'll think it's because of Prince William.

Why's she so upset anyway, she didn't even know Diana, she just liked her because she's all girly and wore dresses. She thinks it's every girl's dream to marry a prince. But I hate frills and make-up and I hate the clothes she buys me, especially the underwear. She doesn't know but on the weekends I wear a pair of boys underpants that I stole from Marks and Spencer. I wash them every Sunday evening and dry them with my hairdryer. And I'm teaching myself to wee standing up. Can't believe I used to think that my missing bits were just trapped inside and would shake loose if I jumped up and down enough times. Mum just thought I loved the trampoline.

I wonder if she remembers that day at the beach when I said I wanted to be a boy. She made some dumb Pinocchio joke and told me I'd lose all my friends.

What friends? Girls think I'm stupid because I act like a boy and boys think I'm stupid because I act like them. I hate when they call me lesbo and dyke at school, I know I'm not gay, I don't know what I am, some kind of freak. Library's useless, can't use the computer because they track everything and there's no-one like me in the biology text books, except that one where some kid drew a cartoon penis on a girl's body.

I wish Dad was still here. He always said "Catherine, you can be anything you want to be when you grow up." Bet he didn't mean a boy though.

Can't stay in here, I'll get the letter and pretend I haven't heard about her precious Princess.

(Goes to the door to look out. Closes door quickly)

The letter's gone.

(Touches door handle three times)

STUPID

By Kevin Six, USA

MIRAM is a 15-year-old girl

MIRAM thinks SHE's too smart for the rest of the world and her mom and adults in general. SHE comes to realize that SHE doesn't know what SHE doesn't know about love.

MIRIAM: Boys are stupid! Teachers, for the most part, are stupid too. My mom's stupid but that goes without saying. Not everybody is stupid. I don't want you to think that I'm some dour teenager who hates the world and thinks everyone is stupid for no apparent reason. No, I'm a dour teenager who hates much of the world and thinks a number of people are stupid for very specific reasons...Take Jimmy Dean. (My mom thinks it's just hilarious that I know a boy named Jimmy Dean and won't take anything I say about him seriously). I don't really know why and she won't explain—she just chokes on her Entenmanns Danish and laughs until I leave the breakfast table. Jimmy Dean is stupid for a very specific reason. And that reason is that he used to like me and now he hates me. Or, he hasn't grown out of pulling my hair and kicking me like he did when we were little to show me he liked me. No. Now he says mean things about me. To my face! And it confuses me. And I hate it when I'm confused over a stupid boy. My teachers are stupid, just like my mom is, because they can't remember back to their teenage years. Or because they've seen too many teenagers' problems and are just sensitized to them. Or is it that they do remember their teenage years but were worse than me? Either way, where's the compassion? Where's the hope in a new generation? I mean, isn't it enough that they're leaving us with a planet that is in desperate need of resuscitation? That they're leaving a banking system in shambles? A national debt that I can't calculate and I take Calculus? That they're sitting back and just letting a war machine run the government and maybe soon the world. A war machine, mind you, that will draft me, thanks to that stupid feminism thing that my mom talks so reverently about.

What were the gains of feminism again? Women can vote, still don't earn fair wages, can't keep a job after getting pregnant unless they sue and now can go to war and die for a country that is so screwed up that we can't fix it. And we will probably have to go to war. Me and Jimmy Dean and any of my friends who are stupid enough to go to war or worse - to get drafted - for people who don't even understand us!

Yeah boys are stupid but they have redeeming qualities. Adults...Politicians...Sheep...are stupid and I think it's time I did something about it. I can't wait until I get the vote. I just hope it's not too late.

THE GREAT WALL

By Jo J. Adamson, USA

BRITTA, A sixteen year old girl who challenges her mother's life style

Some time in the middle 1950s. A ladder back chair sits in the center of the room. To the right is a hat rack with a black dress and black cape hanging on it. BRITTA, a sixteen year old girl is watching her mother put on lipstick in the bathroom mirror. After a few moments SHE says:

BRITTA: Mom, don't you ever want to change? You've worn that hairstyle ever since I can remember, and I'm sixteen!

And your dress is so old fashioned. It's 1955!

You don't have to dress like an old lady. You're just 39. Thirty-nine, mom, the age that Jack Benny decided to stop having birthdays.

Say, how old is that man anyway? He must be at least fifty!—What's wrong with the way you are? Well, nothing if you don't mind being in a rut. And a rut is just a shallow grave.

I'm not being critical, but think about it. Everyday you do the same things. Get up in the morning, make breakfast, get dad off to work.

Monday you wash clothes, Tuesday your iron, Wednesday you bake, Thursday—you clean house. What do you do on Friday? Mending?— That's it. I remember that because you put a light bulb in one of dad's holey socks and you sewed it shut.

Cripes, a light bulb! When I think of a light bulb I think of a bright idea.

And my idea of a 'bright idea' is not to mend anyone's socks—what would I do if I got married?

Cripes. I don't want to get married. Marriage to me is nothing but enslavement—-It's more than that?—What? If you and dad are an example of what marriage could be—

(SHE sees that SHE is upsetting her mother, SHE backs down)

Oh, I'm sorry mom, I didn't mean to hurt your feelings—It's just that your life with dad seems so...boring—You never seem to accomplish anything—

Oh, I don't mean that you don't work! Lord knows, what you do in any given week would exhaust a field hand; it's just that you don't do anything that truly matters.

What truly matters?—anything that doesn't smell like frying onions, look like dirty clothes, or feels like bread dough.

(Talks as if SHE's a teacher lecturing a slow student)

What I'm trying to say is—what truly matters is doing something different with your life.

And something different is what Ingrid Bergman did when she left her husband Petter Lindstrom to live with that Italian film director—Yes, she also left her daughter, Pia, but Ingrid was in love. Truly in love.

Think of the courage it took to leave Hollywood and go off with the love of her life, Roberto Rossellini. Isn't that romantic?—you say it would take more courage to stay with her husband and daughter?—Mom, you just don't understand true love.

And I use Ingrid Bergman as an example because you resemble her—don't laugh, you do. Other people say the same thing.

Florence looks just like Ingrid Bergman did in the movie, "Stromboli"
She fell in love with Roberto while making that movie.

I identified with Karin in the movie because she was an outcast on the
island—What?—Coulee Dam is about as far away as an Italian island
as you can get—I know, but I felt her despair being stuck in such a
ugly place—

She was so....so unhappily beautiful.

When the lighthouse keeper tried to help her escape, the volcano
erupts and shoot, she ends up returning to her fisherman husband!—
Too bad Ingrid didn't do that in real life?—she wasn't in love with her
husband.

Anyway, Mom, you're missing my point—You look like Ingrid
Bergman in Stromboli; you have her same natural beauty—and you're
Swedish—You're not Swedish?—Since when?

Grandma Amanda was from Sweden, and grandma is your mother.
Grandma was born in Umea, that little town near Stockholm—Umea
isn't near Stockholm? Where is it then?—Near Lapland—and about
500 miles from Stockholm.

Whatever! My point is you look like a movie star and dress like a
common housewife.

Nothing personal, but I couldn't bear to live like you do. I want to be
surprised by life. If I thought that each day would be like every other,
I'd want to kill to...to....kill myself!—I'm not being melodramatic. It's
how I feel.

You and dad have been married for almost twenty years and you've
never been out of the country!—well except for that time we went to
Banff National Park—What do I call Canada if it's not out of the
country?—A trip from hell.

Dad and you went on the ice walks and we kids sat in the car.

Yes, by choice. Dad said I had my nose stuck in a book from the time we left home, and Denise couldn't spot any boys on the glaciers so walk would be wasted on her—Didn't I find Lake Louise exciting?— Lake Louise was beautiful, but I wouldn't call it exciting.

Exciting is exotic places and locales—it's being far away from home—it's the world that Patsy Cline sings about in "You belong to me—"

(Sings in an out of tune voice)

"See the pyramids along the Nile\Watch the sunrise on a tropic Isle..."

(BRITTA stops singing. SHE laughs)

I can't carry a tune in bucket, but you get the idea, mom. I want to fly the ocean in a silver plane, see the jungle wet with rain—I want, I want—Out. *(Beat.)*

Next year when I graduate, I'm gonna get as far out of this little dust filled town, as physically possible.

I'll be a distant memory for my teachers who smell like blackboard chalk, the church ladies who reek of lavender toilet water, and my friends who marry their boyfriends and have a passel of kids.

What do I want from life?—I thought I just told you—I want a life full of surprises—Not like yours when nothin' out of the ordinary ever happens—

I'd die if all I had to look forward to was seeing the same people every day, cookin' the same meals, washing the same clothes—

(BRITTA turns towards the door)

Mom where are you going?—Don't go. I'm sorry, I didn't mean to sound so—mean—

(Sound of door shutting. BRITTA gets up from chair, goes over to clothes rack, and slips on a dark dress. SHE takes her hair out of the ponytail and fluffs it out. SHE is now an older adult.)

(BRITTA takes the cape, and goes over to the ladderback chair. SHE puts the cape over the chair, and turns it so the back faces the audience.)

(BRITTA stands at her mother's grave.)

My husband and I had just returned from walking the Great Wall when I got the call from Denise at the Crowne Plaza in Beijing.

My sister, who I hadn't seen for over ten years, told me that you had died in your sleep—Your head was turned toward the wall that held our high school graduation pictures. She said you had a smile on your face.

After I hung up, I felt my life collapse like a deflated balloon. I sat frozen to the chair. When was the last time I saw you? Yes, Christmas, 2000.

I remembered that because it was the year we entered the 21st century. At the time you looked a little peaked, but I didn't give it much thought. You'd live forever. You owed it to me. I had more travel stories to share.

My graduation gown was barely back in the box when I left home.

I moved to a city where the electric lights washed out the stars, became a software engineer, and when my biological clock began to keep me up nights, I married a man who liked my 'feisty' spirit. He made it clear, however, he didn't want that 'spirit' imbued in future generations.

He wanted me for myself, and I wanted the same thing.

"Don't you ever want to change?" I once asked you.

It's taken me years to realize that you never answered. But then again, you didn't have to.

There was nothing you wanted to change into. You were happy with your husband, kids, your little house with the blue Hollyhocks climbing the bay window.

Asking you if you ever wanted to change reminds me of the joke about the light bulb and psychologist—with a slight variation of course.

"How many mothers does it take to change a light bulb?"

Give up, Mom?—You're not good at jokes? That's an easy one. You already know the answer.

(Gently kneels and touches 'the ground' where her mother lies.)

"Just one, but the bulb will have to be ready to change."

(BRITTA smiles)

Thank you, Mom, for not falling in love with an Italian film director, and leaving your daughter behind.

Thanks for not racking up frequent flyer miles in a silver plane, or seeing the jungle wet with rain.

(BRITTA becomes serious, perhaps fights back tears)

Thanks for always being there, but most of all. Thank you for not being ready to change.

THE INTERVENTION

An excerpt from "The Diet Monologues"

Published by JAC Publications, used with permission.

By Monica Bauer, USA

LACEY a 16 year old very hip mall rat

LACEY: So, my Mom said I'm supposed to tell you how this whole thing got started. So, like most of the other important events in my life, I guess it got started at the mall. Like, I'm just one of those people that was born to shop. I mean, totally. And my best friend Susie, is, like, totally into shopping as well.

I tried not to say anything as her weight began to creep up, and up, and up. Then she had that embarrassing fitting room thing, where she asked me to help her cover up the fact that she had just blown out the crotch trying on a size 46 Double-Wide pair of Relaxed Fit Levis that were apparently not relaxed enough for her, like, it was disgusting. Totally. Right then and there I decided I'd better put together an intervention. You know, like they have on television, when some poor addict gets the word he's in dire need of a total change, complete overhaul, or else. I even got Suzie's cousin, the priest, to show up, thinking she'd at least have to listen to him. I mean, Father Jerry is like the voice of God, right. Awesome.

But the problem is, I had no idea how to get Susie to go to this thing, you know, it's supposed to be a surprise. But then the most awesome thing happened; Susie's Mom put ME in charge of planning her Sweet Sixteen party. I sent out invitations to all of her friends, and the theme was, "Help Susie Become a Big Loser". Like a baby shower, only this was going to be a Diet Shower. I registered her at the Atkins Center, Jenny Craig, and L.A. Weight Loss, just to make sure she didn't get any duplicate gifts. I mean, I put a lot of time and effort into making this absolutely perfect.

So on the big day, Susie was kinda expecting some kind of party, and when I took her to my house, she was starting to get excited already. So when she walked in the door and we all yelled "Surprise", she looked so happy I knew it was all gonna go great. Then she starts opening her presents. The Low-Carb Cookbook. Thin For Life. Getting Fit the Jenny Craig Way. Melissa, the most popular girl in our school, went all out and got her an entire month's supply of chocolate Slim Fast, which was amazing, because I didn't think she'd even show up, because Melissa doesn't even LIKE Susie all that much.

Then, we all take our turns, getting up. We tell her how much we love her, and that we will all help her every step along the weight-loss way, and, like, Father Jerry even came up with a patron saint for weight loss she could pray to special, which I thought was totally sweet. We're all waiting to hear what Susie is gonna say, and you won't believe it, but, honest to God, she got up all calm and everything, and walked out! She hasn't spoken to me since! I tried to send her an IM the next day, and she spammed me with a ton of diet ads!

Last time I checked my Facebook, I had seventy-five messages about how I could lose weight while sleeping, or drinking green tea, or buying some machine that exercises my abs for me! It is totally clogging my inbox! I don't know what this means!

We have been friends since the second grade, and now she's just become this source of nasty spam. I asked my Mom what I could possibly have done wrong, and she said, "Lacey, you should go out and do some research." About being fat! Which is totally bizarre, because I've never had a weight problem in my life.

I didn't know where to start, so Mom gave me a list of people she wanted me to see. Way weird!

RENDER

By Mary O'Malley, USA

RACHEL is a pretty 17 year old dressed in a quirky vintage way

SHE is enraged and trapped in the middle of argument with mother in a suburban kitchen in late May, the day before her high school graduation.

RACHEL: Leave, why don't you just leave. Drive to Canada again. Go psycho again. Search for the aliens who will rescue your stupid ass. You didn't have the decency to get Breast Cancer like Aunt Jeanne. Everyone helped her out. Flowers and dinners, they even took a family trip to Europe before she died! They called her a saint and she is a saint. Your nothing compared to her. Only gave me bad genes. Do you know what my friends say about you? How weird you are. How weird you talk not making sense or not saying anything at all. Can you even carry on a normal conversation like Sammi's mom or April's mom? You walk around with no bras. Well you did. I don't have sleep-overs because of you. Don't bring Blake home because of you. Don't bother to come to graduation. I'll walk right past you. So cry if you want! You never thought about me when you left last summer. Did you know how Dad looked in the morning? All gray faced and dead looking calling Grandma and Mrs. Woodburn, trying to figure out what crazy escape plan you hatched. He called the fuckin' Erie Benedictines to see if you had gone all holy and hermit like again. You should've booked a flight to Borneo. It was so considerate of you to come back. Didn't stay home long did you? How many days were you in the hospital last year Mom? Did you miss us, did you think of us? Might have been half way around the world. I heard they kept you locked up. Just like a jail. No I won't stop it. Yeah, I need a shrink, probably need some meds so I can zone out just like you. Walk around in pj's all day. Yeah I remember. But I don't think about the past. I had a good mother She had a cool job, we had money. I had horse riding and voice lessons. Everybody liked her. She used to take me shopping for clothes at Abercrombie and Forever 21. But she's dead. What did you tell me the Jews do when they cut some one off? Sit Shiva? Well I prayed. I cried. I burnt your pictures and poems in the fireplace on the patio. Sang funeral songs all by myself. I pulled my hair out, cut holes in my clothes. Yeah, I really, really did. I'm still Catholic, still go to Mass; haven't gone Buddhist like you. I buried her memory in my brain, I imagine her soul is in purgatory forever. Her image gone from my mind like the last firework on the 4th of July. Too bad loser. Would you just stop looking at me like that? You never should've tried to divorce Dad. I can say what I want! I know more things than you. Yeah your fuckin' right I do. He tells me I'm more adult than you. You don't deserve him. Sure he treats you like a child. He has to. You're the one who ruined the family. No, I won't shut up. You listen to me. Stop crying and go to your room.

THE UNWANTED GUEST

By Nina Solomita, USA

DAUGHTER, 17 years old

(Notes: The lines in italics are parts of songs and should be sung or spoken in sing-song fashion. The daughter is meant to speak all the mother's lines as well as her own.)

DAUGHTER: My mom says her heart is on the mend, though *it will take some time this time.* She speaks in verse—bits of songs, words we've heard but may not know from where or when. When she says her heart is on the mend, I see her big fat heart in my mind's eye, a stitch here, a stitch there, to hold the poor torn halves in place. Then the stitches melt and fade, the new weave blends with the old, leaving just a hint of a scar. This sight makes me smile, and Mom asks what the hell is that smirk for?

I don't laugh at her. It's just that, to me, a heart is a pump, no more, no less. These cracks, breaks and tears live in the mind not the chest.

Since Pete died, she plays the part of the child and me the part of the mom. Five years. From one day to the next she changed. A still cold fear filled in the blue of her eyes and stuck, like a guest who came for an hour but stayed on and on and then moved in for good. Each day I check her eyes. I don't lose hope that one day the guest will leave and my old true mom will come back. Until then, I must be the wise one.

She pouts. Her lower lip pulls her face to the ground. Her red nails drum a beat, and she sings, *I'm gonna lock my heart and throw away the key.*

I say while you're at it, you should *wash that man right out of her hair.* This brings a trace of a smile. The man she cries for was a no-good like the rest, here one day, gone the next, my mom a soft place to rest his head. They're all the same to me. I wish she'd stop the search. It goes nowhere.

No man hits her. She's firm on that. But they do hurt her each time. They take—steal, I call it—use her up and throw her out. Why won't you learn, I ask?

I have to try, she says. *Some day he'll come along, the man I love.* He may be just round the next bend and what if I missed him?

I tell her, you have to find her own way, a man can't save you. But I don't think she hears this at all. She still waits for Pete to come back in some new form.

No man will make me sad, I say. No man will make me cry.

She says, you'll change your tune one day. *Some day your prince will come.*

I laugh at this. Where is your prince? I say. Then I know I've gone too far. I know not to look in her eyes now. It will be too sad, even for me.

As you see, I can be mean. I don't want to, but there are times when I can't help it. It's when I get fed up, when I want to stop the talk that leads nowhere, the same old talk we go through all the time that takes us around in circles. I want to open a door and walk out instead of going round in circles with mom.

Soon I will tell her I must leave. With this act, I hope she grows up. It's tough love. I've read this term, and it makes a lot of sense to me. I know I'll have to be strong, that it will be hard, but how else will she learn? After Pete died, she went on strike from life's chores. Although she has a job, I do the rest. When I go, she will have to cook, clean, buy her own clothes. She has to learn. Again!

For my part, I need to *break the chains that bind me*. When high school ends, I want a place of my own. My plan is to work days and go to school nights, read, learn. Then I want to see the world. Go to

Greece. Stretch my wings like a bird, dip and soar and feel the wind carry me away.

We shop at K-Mart. She picks a blouse the shade of an egg yolk, a skirt the shade of a grape—to my mind a bad choice, but I let it go. I don't let her see, try as she might, what I feel about the clothes. My face is a mask. From now on she will shop alone. She pulls a dress from the rack and says, "What do you think of this?" Like a dog, she smells something is up.

I am calm. What do you think? I say.

Her eyes are slits. I like it, she says.

Fine, I say. You see, she can do it if she has to. Tough love works. Each day I try one small new thing to get her ready to hear my news. It won't be long now. I have to face the music and dance. We both do.

I choose a day in June. One week before the end of school, I will tell her. I set the scene in my mind's eye like a play. I learn my lines. But when the day comes I am tense. My mouth is dry; it's hard to speak. Tough love, I say to myself, tough love.

I come home from school. She sits on the couch, her feet in a blue basin. She says she likes her work, but her feet don't. Each afternoon she soaks them in salts. When we're in the mood, I dry them with a soft towel and then rub them. We have not done this for a while. She looks at me, smiles. Hi, Sweets, she says. Want to rub my poor feet? Today it would be better not to rub her feet, better for me. But she hands me the towel. She flirts with me.

Okay, I say. I kneel. I take the towel, pull one foot out and dry it, then the other. I squeeze out some skin cream and rub it onto her skin. As I look down at her foot in my hands, I have a funny quick thought that her foot is holding my hand. I feel something press down in my throat. It makes my face hot. My mom purrs. Most times I like this sound, but now, today, I don't want to hear it. Quick! Hurry! Tell her quick. I make haste with her feet and replace her slippers. I stand and take a few steps back. Her eyes are on her feet. Mine now see the top of her scalp, pink, through her hair. The sound in my ears is my heartbeat. Time to dive in. Time to face the music. Time to dance.

Mom, I need to move out. I need to live on my own. The words are out; the ball rolls—no stopping it now. Her head stays down; she does not move. Her feet have her full attention, and it seems we both don't breathe.

Then she lifts her head. We catch eyes and her face breaks—mouth, nose, cheeks, jump. I make my face stone. It does not move, it can't. I must be strong. This is the best way. It's up to me.

Why? What have I done?

You haven't done anything. It's just that... For a moment, I forget my lines. It's just that we need...we're too close. It's not good for us.

What's not good? Being close is good. We all need to be close to someone, we all need someone to love. Nothing wrong with that. We help each other. You help me, I help you. That's life.

But mom, the way we help each other...it's not the best way, it holds us back.

So I hold you back, do I?

We both do it, mom. I hold you back too.

(Silence)

I need my own place. So do you. We need a change. I want to branch out, do new things...You can be different, happier—better than you are now, but not with me here.

What's gotten into you? I don't need to be…different! Did you get this out of one of your books? I'm in your way, is that it? Is that what you think? Your old mom's in your way?

It's not that…I feel my feet grow roots through the floor and down into the ground.

What is it then? What is it? Why are you talking like this?

Tears perch on her eyelids. To see her now, my heart hurts. I hear its sad beat turn into a moan. My heart beats its sad song with hers, which is on the mend, and I hope that mine too will mend some day. In my mind's eye, I see a line drawn that ties me to her and her to me and us to all the hearts that are sad, that swell with hurt, that float like blimps in the sky—big, sad, fat red hearts tied in a bright red line.

I don't want to see this. I want to remember tough love. But our hearts are in the way. They block my view. She feels me shift. Her eyes work on me.

You know, honey, you don't have to leave to get what you want. You can do it here. I can see why you want more. I can. And *we can work it out*. Her voice soothes like a hymn. Don't worry. We'll work it out. Everything will be all right. Really.

With these words, she sounds like a true grown up, and I want to curl up in her arms.

Let's not talk about this anymore today. You think about it. Tomorrow we'll talk again. You can tell me what you want. Things can change. I can change. You'll see.

That night I go to sleep and dream. I'm ten. It's six o'clock and Pete, my dad, is due home to eat. Mom cooks. The roast beef spills its juice with a hiss and fills the air with thick, warm smells. I am setting the table. Mom looks at me and smiles, the blue of her eyes clear and bright. Her red heels click on the floor as she walks over and hugs me tight. You're doing a good, job, Sweets, she says. I swell with pride, but to hide the flush on my cheek, I bow my head and place a fork just so. Mom's arm rests on my waist, her cheek a touch on mine.

ME AND THE RAIN

From "Living Dolls"

By Elaine Romero, USA

SOFIA, 18, a runaway, Latina

(Lights up on SOFIA, a waifish-looking, Latina in her late teens. SOFIA has been wearing the same clothes for three days and it shows. SHE sits next to the window, leaning against it from time to time. The sound of light rain.)

(SOFIA looks down at the table.)

SOFIA: "Me and the Rain." I've been sitting here in this twenty-four hour cafe for three days now. I've established myself at a certain table. I leave my stuff here when I go to the bathroom or get up to stretch. My table's next to a window. *(SHE looks out the window.)* I'm safe here. 'Cause the people who are looking for me—they don't look very hard.

(Beat) The owner, he's been real nice. Sometimes, I think I'm here just so I can be close to him. He cleans up after the people when they leave. He's always shoving little bits of paper into his back pocket. He makes you feel good. The way he takes control. Not like home. Where the people scream until their throats bleed. Just 'cause it makes 'em feel better. To be bleeding. 'Cause blood makes you feel real. The way it pours straight out of your veins.

(SHE sighs) The owner smiles when I catch his eye. I think he likes having me here. Especially, during the rough times. When nobody else's here. He's the kind of person who needs people. You can tell. He lights up like a match when they come in. And it's not just a money thing 'cause sometimes they just want to use the phone, or the toilet, and he always lets them.

(Beat) He called me behind the counter today for a little conversation. At first I was sort of scared 'cause I thought he was gonna send me away. Turns out, he noticed I was down to my last two dollars. He asked me if I'd start working in exchange for coffee. I think he's really trying to help, but I don't know if he wants something else. *(Avoiding the thought, SHE looks out the window.)*

(Beat) It's been raining these last two days. Rain makes you feel safe 'cause it covers you. The whole you. Rain has a way of slipping down inside the openings of your clothes. Of touching you even when it never hits your skin. I love the rain. 'Cause it's okay to cry. Outside in the rain. See, everybody thinks it's just the rain in your eyes. The rain blends with your tears and you can't tell what came first. Your tears or the rain.

(Beat) Gloria, that's my identical twin sister. She drives by here at least once a day. Mom's got her out there looking for me—only Gloria's not really looking. *(Beat)* They call us identical, but there's nothing identical about us. I don't think we've ever thought anything alike. Like, now. She insists on looking in the wrong places. On the street. On the sidewalk. She doesn't think to look inside.

(Beat) And mom, she's no help. She wouldn't dare look herself. Maybe she can't. Her eyes—they're real cloudy. From all the drinking she's been doing. *(Beat)* When Gloria and I were little girls, she'd step through the clouds once in awhile. She hasn't found her way out in a real long time. And I'm yelling, "Mom. Hey, Mom. I'm here." But she doesn't see me anymore. *(SOFIA looks down at the table.)* "Color me with angst." That's what someone wrote on the table. I'm not sure what it means, but it sounds right. I'm afraid if that's what angst is. Afraid of all sorts of things. That the rain's gonna stop. That my sister'll give up on me. That the owner's gonna kick me out. I'm afraid to stand up. 'Cause once I walk out, I'll have to decide. Thing after thing. Hard things and small things. Things that might not really matter, but they feel like they do. *(The sound of the light rain stops.)* I'm afraid of staying here forever. Of seeing someone who knows me. Of getting lost in the background and no one knowing me anymore.

(Beat) The rain just stopped. It's always quiet. That split second after the rain. The silence—it means something. You're supposed to make up your mind. Make a decision. What kind of decision? The right one. The best one for yourself. No pressure. Just be perfect and don't make mistakes. 'Cause you only live once. *(SOFIA crosses to the door.)* The street still looks wet. And it's quiet. Like in the middle of the night. Except it's not. The owner is talking to one of his employees. There isn't going to be any last smile from him. *(SOFIA takes a deep breath.)* Fresh air. It's pulling me outside. *(SOFIA steps outside.)* The rain says hello. Just a sprinkle at first. It's inviting me to take another step. *(SHE does.)* So, I lift up my arms and let it pour. On me—the rain. I hold it close and it holds me. I take it with me. It's okay to cry now 'cause I have the rain. *(SOFIA exits.)*

KATIE KNOWS

From "Red Rover"

By Michèle Raper Rittenhouse, USA

KATIE is eighteen years old

SHE is in Mississippi 1969 in her Grandmother May's kitchen. SHE is leaving for college in a few weeks and has just discovered that her brother, Robbie, is missing in action in Vietnam. SHE is presently trying on a college gift, a ball gown, when SHE hears the news.

KATIE: But...just missing means...they...can't find...his body...so... he...might not be dead. So without a body, he could be alive....somewhere in the... in the jungle... maybe wounded... or...or...captured. Or maybe he's just hiding from them. He's fine and he's hiding. And when he gets his chance, he'll make his way back to the base and all his buddies will celebrate and we'll get a letter from him, any day now, telling us about his adventure and how they all laughed when he got back and how...stupid the Viet Cong were to miss him while he was hiding in a........in a dead tree or something, and how they walked past him and didn't even see him, just like he did with me when we played hide and seek in the woods out back and if he can fool me, he can fool them, outsmart them, and survive and get away and.....and.....make it home. Make it back home. What a story, mama, what a story that's going to be. Don't you see? That's what's happening. He's fine. I know he's fine. I can feel that he's fine. He's laughing right now, thinking how he's going to tell us about what happened. I can hear him laugh right now....I can hear him....(*Stops. Looks at her dress*) It seems so strange, where he is and where we are...appears to be so different. But it's all the same, isn't it. My ball gown, his jungle, it's the same, it happens at the very same time, on the very same planet, and only....only a distance separates us. But it's the same time...........So you see, I know. I know he's alright. He's fine. Just as if he were here with us now.....fine.

حم

RAISON D'ETRA

From "Sweet Potato Pie for Sheila Aretha Tucker"

By Bara Swain, USA

SHEILA ARETHA TUCKER, age 19

SHEILA returns home to Tennessee during Spring Break, 2005, and to her "perpetually grieving mother" over the death of her father.

AT RISE: SHEILA looks up from her textbook and addresses the audience.

SHEILA: Is Mama tellin' you her life story now? *(SHE closes her book.)* And did she get to the part where my daddy gets down on his knee to ask for her hand in marriage? *(SHE gives the audience a "thumbs up")* And has she told you that Grandmother Graves gave her a phonograph as a shower gift and an electric typewriter for a wedding present? *(after a moment)* Well, you can still find them both in the family room downstairs. The phonograph is in a sideboard from old Mrs. Duffy that my father stripped and sanded and stained in a cool blonde oak. My daddy loved his blondes! And Mother's favorite poster is still hanging above it, too: *McGovern for President: Come Home America, 1972.* I had it laminated for her last birthday. I also gave her a parakeet named Philip, after Philip Norman Bredesen, the 48th governor of Tennessee and, Mama says, a potential contender for the 2008 Democratic nomination for President. Woo hoo! *(SHE laughs)* Mother's pet bird, unfortunately, developed vertigo from a vitamin deficiency and died after several...well, many!...many falls from his perch. My perpetually bereaved mother wrapped him in one of her dingy pillowcases from "her marriage bed," she said, and buried the keet among her favorite wild irises. They were Daddy's favorite, too. (pause) And as for the ancient Smith Corona from Grandmother Graves, Mother keeps it on her ironing board next to a set of World Book Encyclopedias and an overstuffed couch, also compliments of old Mrs. Duffy. In fact, that eccentric old woman bequeathed her entire—although modest—estate to my parents when she passed on in 1988. Daddy sold her house in Union City and made some investments "for our future," he said. *(SHE raises her eyebrows)* For our future, he said. That's an interesting concept, you see, because Mother lives only for the past and the present, whereas I live for...I live for...*(SHEILA pauses)* That's a...convoluted question. Who wants to know, anyway? *(SHE scans the audience for someone to acknowledge her. No one does)* Alright, then. Here's a burning question that I have for you. Let's have a show of hands, please. Has Mama told you the results of her latest cholesterol screening? Because I have it from the horse's mouth that her HDL is the same as Grandmother Graves' property taxes, and her LDL is higher than Clingmans Dome near Gatlinberg, Tennessee. And that's the third highest point in the whole god-damned Appalachian mountain range! Oh! She drives me crazy! "Didn't you write the figure down, Mother?" I asked. And she answered, "No, I did not write the 'figger' down, Sheila. But I wrote a limerick about Great Uncle Jimmy's gout. Do you want to hear it?" *(SHE plugs her own ears and closes her eyes)* No, Mother. I do not want to hear it. Just like I did not...relish her recitation about lactic acid and Lambda particles and the Lewis and Clarke expedition. Or her description of leprosy or the topography of Libya or the reign of Louis the Pious, and Louis the First and Louis the Second and...*(SHEILA's jaw drops open)*...And Mama is reading volume "L" this week. *(SHE explains)* The World Book Encyclopedia. Volume "L"! Mama reads while she's doing the laundry. Then she jots down her ideas or stories or random facts while she's ironing her shirts—for "prosperity," Mama says—which is as articulate as "you betcha, you betcha!" and as perceptive as "It's cold enough to freeze the balls off a pool table." Lord help us all, she has a weakness for utterly useless trivia, too. Like...did you know that a coat hanger is 44 inches long if straightened, and that a housefly hums in the middle octave, key of F? Or has Mama mentioned that you are more likely to be killed by a champagne cork than a poisonous spider, or that Ulysses S. Grant smoked 20 cigars a day? *(SHE pauses)* Did Mama tell you how she tried to quit smoking after daddy had his first heart attack? Or how she called me their "raison d'etra!"...even on my father's deathbed! *(In a sudden outburst)* Why did she have to be so damned selfish! I mean, why couldn't she have given me a brother or a sister...anything!...so that I wouldn't have to be so god damned special! *(SHE can't bring herself to look at anyone.)* I don't want so much responsibility. *(SHE looks up)* I don't want it.

HOW FAMILY IS MADE

By Barbara Lindsay, USA

SERENA, a young woman (late teens - early 20s), remembers her turmoil over her mother's remarriage

SERENA: The day my mother got married again was the worst day of my life. I was nine and I was powerless. In fact, that was the day I found out just how powerless I was. I didn't want any of what was happening, but I couldn't stop it, either. I didn't want my father to be sad. I didn't want my mother to look at another man the way she looked at her new husband. I didn't want to stand next to them in front of everybody and answer their questions about how I would join with them to make a new family. And I didn't want a brother. But there he was. He was fifteen, and he scared me. His hair was long and thick and he was pierced in strange places. His eyes always seemed to be half closed and he never said what he was thinking. I wanted my mother to protect me from him, but my mother didn't seem to see anything except this man she was marrying. The times I was at my mother's house, when we had dinner, I always had to sit next to my new brother. I didn't like that. I didn't like the things I felt when I looked at his big arms. My sister was young enough that she could cry and throw tantrums, so sometimes they allowed her to stay with my father. But I couldn't do that. I didn't know how. So I went to my mother's house and played with my toys and watched videos. I tried to be a family. But I didn't know how to do that either. Later, much later, after he had left the house and was living at college, I found out that my stepbrother was a good person. He has a very big heart. And even later, I realized that he was quiet and dark because he was powerless, too. I don't know how I saw that. We never talked about it. I guess families are made in all kinds of ways. I would do anything for him now. But we don't see him much. Maybe I was lucky that I was only nine. It's easier to bend and take new shapes when you're still growing. It might have helped if I had known that. There's so much I want to say to him now, to say to all of them, my mother, too. I don't know how. But I'm going to try.

MATERNITY

By Barbara Lindsay, USA

PAULA, a young (teens to 20s) mother to be

PAULA reflects on her approaching motherhood.

PAULA: I didn't think it was possible. I had no idea. That's what makes it a miracle, isn't it. I've loved people before. I love her father. I love him more now than I did when I found out I loved him in the first place. But this isn't like that. I know it isn't because I don't think of him as my husband any more. He's her father to me now. Without even meaning to, that's how I think of him. Her father. My baby's father. My daughter's father. My daughter. I'm so—happy. I don't know how else to say it. I'm so eager to hold her, I can hardly sit still for a minute, and I know I must be smiling when I sleep. I know it; I can tell. I want to look at her, and talk to her, and kiss her sweet, soft, baby skin, and feel her wispy little baby breath, and nurse her. Especially that. That must be nice. That must be nicer than almost anything in the world. Still, it's hard to think of her outside of me, in the world. Sometimes I wish I could keep her here. She's safe now. I don't drive any more. There's nowhere I want to go. I'm so careful when I reach, or when I bend. Everything I touch, I touch lightly, and if there's something I can't do, I just don't do it. I don't care. And I'm feeding her all sorts of wonderful things. I eat carrots and chew them up very, very fine, and just before I swallow, I say a little prayer. "Here's for your eyes," I say, or "Here's for your skin or your muscles or your bones or your little beating heart." I don't think the real God minds that the prayers aren't to Him. He knows what's important. I listen to the best music all the time. When I hear a rap song, I just turn around and walk away. Somewhere I read that babies like cello music and organ music, so I listen to those. I sit near the speaker in the rocking chair and try to rock in time to the music. That way she'll be able to dance. Her father can't dance at all. I think his mother must have listened to garbage trucks and Saturday morning cartoons. That's

50

what it's like when he dances. My daughter will be able to dance. My daughter. My baby.

PHONE HOME

From "Sleep/Speak"

By Sera Weber-Striplin, USA

Original Production, University of Akron, 2004

ACTOR who plays both *ACTOR* and *MOM*

ACTOR: I once heard that we become simpler late at night. Through exhaustion, we lose all the complications that wall us up in an image. It's sort of like we unglue from all of our hang-ups and insecurities, and we're just people.

It's only late at night that I become this way. I just have to tell someone what's on my mind or...I feel like I'm still too complicated. There's one person I know I can always talk to, even this late at night.

MOM: Hello?

My Mom.

ACTOR: Hi Mom.

It doesn't matter what time I call. She's always willing to talk to me.

MOM: How are you, dear? How is school?

Now is the time to say what I have to say.

ACTOR: Mom, I'm failing all my classes.

MOM: You'll figure it out.

My Mom is nearly impervious to shock. Even at this hour of the night. Even when she's at her most vulnerable state.

ACTOR: *Mom, I'm dropping out.*

MOM: *Well, take a semester off, sweetie. No one said ya couldn't.*

It's not that I don't appreciate it. It's just the opposite really. I'm sure I could tell her anything and she'd be behind me...Which is why I sometimes feel the need to...test it.

ACTOR: *I'm calling you from jail, Mom.*

MOM: *Oh...You young kids always getting into mischief. (pause)*

ACTOR: *I was fired from my job yesterday.*

MOM: *You can talk to Uncle Vic about finding a job at the plant.*

(pause)

ACTOR: *I got into an accident last night.*

MOM: *I'm glad you're okay.*

(pause)

ACTOR: *Mah, Ron and I are pregnant.*

MOM: *That's wonderful. When are you due?*

(short pause)

ACTOR: *We're getting married...in Vegas...tomorrow.*

MOM: *I'll come.*

(shorter pause)

ACTOR: *I joined a gang.*

MOM: Be careful.

ACTOR: I got a nipple piercing.

MOM: Neato.

ACTOR: -a tattoo.

MOM: Wow.

ACTOR: I'm gay!

(a brief pause indicates a possible victory, before a complete denial)

MOM: Good fer you.

(pause)

ACTOR: Well, I'll talk to you tomorrow, Mom.

MOM: All right, honey. Goodnight.

(silence)

Goodnight.

Good night. I'm not sure we appreciate "good night." It means to wish somebody a moment of the uncomplicated. Or several. And that's pretty extraordinary.

It's good to know that you have someone, who you can depend on to unwind you from the complex. Every night...Good night.

ROSIE, THE TEDDY BEAR

By Steven Bergman, USA

ROSIE, 15-25 years old and dressed in a fuzzy life-size teddy bear suit

Place: The side of a highway road. Dirt and gravel on the ground. Time: Present.

ROSIE: (*ROSIE is laying down on the stage in a contorted position. SHE addresses the audience:*) Hi there. Nice to see you. How am I? Feeling a little down, but other than that, I'm doing okay. You found me here lying by the side of the road. I bet you didn't know that the breeze of passing cars can actually be refreshing at times. Don't think so? Well, that's probably cause if you stop on a highway, chances are something is wrong. But it's true - I know. (*Pause.*) I hear one coming now...here it comes...whoosh! (*SHE wobbles from side to side.*) That felt pretty goo...ow! Unless, of course, you forget about the rip in your arm. It can sting a little if the breeze gets TOO strong. I could probably use some stitches, but I don't know when that's gonna happen. I've been here through two light times and two dark times. I don't get nearly as lonely during the light times as I do during the dark times, because I can see what's going on. During the dark time, I can never tell if something will come around to check me out. In the light time, I can see them coming by to sniff me, and even though it's comforting to be able to see, all I think about is "please don't take my stuffing, please don't take my stuffing, PLEASE DON'T TAKE MY STUFFING!" During the last light time, a small, furry animal came to check me out. He got up real close, and I could feel his warm breath on my tummy as he sniffed me. He tried to nudge me, to see if I was alive and would move or something. You would think that real animals would be smarter than teddy bears, but it appears not, since I obviously was NOT going to move for him. So when I didn't move for him, he put his teeth in my arm and threw me back and forth a couple of times, like this (*SHE flings herself as if being tossed around by the animal*).

And that's how I got the rip in my arm. Oh, don't worry, it's not the first rip I've had. I've had this happen to me before: when the Little Girl was tiny, she would swing me and throw me around all the time. I was newer then, so I stayed together much better than I do now. But one time she threw me into a wall, and my eye popped off. It didn't hurt too much (I'm well—padded), I just couldn't see very well until the Bigger Lady took out a small sharp object, put a piece of string through it, and put my eye back on. I felt good as new after that. But now it's been many dark times and many light times, and I'm starting to get frayed, so that stupid animal's teeth opened the hole in my arm. I wish the Bigger Lady was here to stitch it up, but I know she won't be.

The Little Girl got me as a present before she could even talk. A Big Boy found me in a trashcan (a little dirty, but still new in my box) and brought me to where the Little Girl and the Bigger Lady lived. "I got ya something for your kid!" he said, and tossed me on the table. So the Bigger Lady opened me up and placed me next to the Little Girl while she slept. It was very nice. The Little Girl looked so peaceful lying there sleeping in the dark times, and just looking around and making all sorts of cute cooing and gurgling noises during the light times. That was the happiest time of my life. The swinging phase was not a lot of fun, but I saw the pleasure it gave the Little Girl, so getting tossed around didn't matter much to me. As the Little Girl got bigger, she stopped throwing me around so much. Instead, she would hug me and squeeze me and talk to me all the time. During the light times, she would ask my thoughts about what-to-do's, why's and where-to-go's. "Should we have water or tea with our snack, Rosie?" or "Where do you think we should go today, Rosie?" or "Do you think Mommy's gonna have any visitors today, Rosie?" Rosie - that's my name. When the Little Girl would get upset, she'd call me Rosie Rosie, but most of the time, she just called me Rosie. She called me that because I have a rose in the center of my tummy - she told me so herself. It was a nice name - I liked it. I knew when she used it that she was talking to me. There were dark times when she would say things like, "Don't listen to what she's saying, Rosie Rosie!" "If we put our hands over our ears, we won't hear what they're saying, Rosie Rosie" or "Maybe if I stay here, she won't find me, Rosie Rosie," and then the Bigger Lady would come into the room and she wouldn't be acting like she did when she fixed my eye - oh, no. She would start to say very loud things that I couldn't understand because she connected all her words together, like (*SHE stands up to imitate the "Bigger Lady" shouting*) "How-many-times-have-i-told-you-not-to-come-out-when-i-have-company? If-someone-sees-you-we-won't-get-any-money-for-food?!?" Then the Bigger Lady would take the Little Girl away from me and leave me in the dark. I couldn't see, but I could hear the loud sounds, and the sounds would pierce my stuffing all the way through my body as the Little Girl screamed for the Bigger Lady to stop what she was doing. Finally, the Little Girl would come back to me, her face wet with streams of tears, and she would want to talk to me very much. "One day, Rosie Rosie, you and I will run away from here, and then she'll be sorry!" or "Oh, Rosie Rosie, I just need you to kiss this one spot on my arm, cause I know your teddy bear kisses will help it feel better." I would always give her my teddy bear kisses whenever she asked.

This isn't the first time I've been outside the house. Sometimes the Little Girl and I would go out with the Bigger Lady to different places. But most of the time, we just went to the "Old Woman's." The Bigger Lady would take us there, and say, "Time to stay with the Old Woman until I get back to get you!" The Old Woman never played with us, she would just sit there and leave the Little Girl and I in a room with a movie box. We just sat there, no one saying a word. Then finally we would hear the Bigger Lady outside. "Get out here, now! It's time to go home!" We would get back in the car, and go back home. No one would say a word, except when the Little Girl would whisper songs to me in the back seat of the car. They always made me smile.

On (*fill in the day two days ago*), the Bigger Lady came into our room and said, "Come-on-now-we're-gonna-go-see-the-Old-Woman-let's-go-don't-be-slow!" in the loud slurry voice that was hard to understand. So we got in the car. I knew the feelings of the road from our house to the Old Woman's pretty well, but today the curves and bumps seemed bigger than usual. The Bigger Lady was saying words about the car, about the Old Woman, and about other people I had never heard of. And then all of a sudden, the car made a very big bump, and lots of high, loud noises, and everything in the car started moving around all over the place. I could hear the Bigger Lady shouting words I couldn't understand, and the last thing I heard the Little Girl say was, "Rosie Rosie!" before I was thrown out of the car and into the air. I landed on the road right near where you see me now. I wanted so badly to see where the Little Girl had gone to, but I was facing the wrong direction! Then it became very quiet, and then...BOOM!!! I didn't feel anything, but it sounded like the BOOM was not too far off in the distance. Oh, I really want to hear, "Oh, Rosie, its time to go home now to our room." But so far, the Little Girl hasn't come to get me. I don't understand it, but I will be strong, as the Little Girl has been strong, and I will wait here until she finds me...

END OF PLAY

MASHED POTATOES

By Virginia (Ginger) Fleishans, USA

A YOUNG MOTHER

At a family dinner, a YOUNG MOTHER had been mashing potatoes when SHE suddenly ran into the back yard shouting and cursing in a fit of temper. Later, at home that evening, SHE tries to explain her actions to her daughter who is in an infant carrier.

YOUNG MOTHER: Here we are, sweetheart. You sit there and I'll sit here in this rocker and we'll see if we can't calm down together. Whew! Doesn't it feel good to sit down for a few minutes? I don't get to enjoy the patio very often. It's lovely out here. Mm-mm. This is good brandy.

It wasn't your fault, or your brothers', and I'm not angry with you. Sometimes I get so overwhelmed I just can't hold it in.

We weren't even supposed to have mashed potatoes tonight. But at 6 o'clock, Daddy came into the kitchen and says, "You are going to make mashed potatoes to go with Nancy's beautiful gravy, aren't you?" So what could I do? Nancy, perfect Aunt Nancy, was in the middle of a vanilla pastry cream so she certainly couldn't do it. Could I tell him I was about to open a bag of frozen fries? Of course not—so I started peeling. And peeling. And peeling. After all, there were 11 of us.

And I couldn't tell him that I still have 16 measures of Sonata Pathetique to memorize before Thursday either! *(Groan.)* I think I need a little more of that brandy. So I got them all peeled, and cooked. And I was just starting to mash them when he came in again. And the second time he said, well you were there. You heard the whole thing. I'm sure he wasn't trying to push me over the edge. But when I shouted "Enough! Enough enough enough enough enough!" and ran out the back door, he didn't know what hit him!

What's a matter? Hmm? Oh! You lost your binkie. Oops! Here. Here it is.

And then when I really got mad and started saying "Fu...," well, again, you were there and heard that too. I am sorry I said that. But, I'll never forget the look on his and Nancy's faces when I started screaming at the top of my lungs. And crying. Then, everybody else had to come out and gape.

You seen, he thinks I told the quartet I couldn't play anymore because of moving and Grandpa's dementia and the new puppies. Ha! If that were all I had to worry about, there'd be no problem. But with you (but not really, because you are the only bright spot in my life!) and your brothers' soccer games and homework and dirty laundry and baseballs that fly into neighbor's windows, and cooking three meals— well, two meals and brown bag lunches, really—and dirty laundry and mending and doctor's appointments and oh, did I mention that the ignition sticks on the car sometimes?

Did you lose it again? Here it is. I should rinse it off...here, I'll just dip it in my glass. Mm-mm. It's blackberry. What do you think? Yeah, I like it too.

Oh, God! If anyone had told me eight years ago that I'd be still be practicing a piece two days before a performance, I wouldn't have believed them. All gone. All gone! Maybe just a little more.

It was funny though when I started feeling the ant bites. There I was, having a nervous breakdown in the middle of an ant hill! And what did I do? Couldn't help it—it was so "me..." just so darned funny to think I even messed that up...I couldn't stop laughing. But let me tell you, those bites really itch now.

To Constance! For introducing me to brandy. Did you know it comes in flavors: apple, apricot, blackberry, plum, raspberry? That makes it sound more like fruit, or fruit juice maybe.

Do you think mommy is nuts? Yeah, me too. Sometimes. When you grow up, you might go crazy too. Someday. I love you so much. So much. I love you. I do.

CANTALOUPES

By Christy A. Brothers, USA

VICKI, in her twenties, in her mother's hospital room

VICKI is in a hospital room visiting her mother who suffered a heart attack a few hours before VICKI's arrival. SHE is wearing her pajamas and looks like SHE just rolled from bed. SHE has a blanket wrapped around herself and is talking to the cardiologist. Her state of mind is somewhat manic from shock and exhaustion. Her mother is sleeping.

VICKI: She looks so good. God, I can't believe how good she looks. I didn't know what to expect. I drove two hours to get here so I could see her for myself and all kinds of horrible images kept popping into my head. I just didn't know what........I didn't know how she'd look. I haven't even brushed my teeth or changed my clothes. I just heard my sister say 'Don't freak out' on the other end of the phone. Don't freak out. Was she kidding me? Don't freak out. Wouldn't you freak out? Of course I freaked out. It was 2:30 in the morning. Everyone freaks out when the phone starts ringing in the middle of the night. When the phone rang, I thought it might be my sister needing to talk because she had another fight with her boyfriend, but it wasn't. Yeah, it was my sister, but it wasn't about boyfriends. I just knew it wasn't. You know how you know stuff sometimes, you just have feelings about stuff. I just knew something. I knew someone was either dead or seriously close to being dead. It's amazing how in a few seconds you see everyone you've ever loved in caskets. Sick, isn't it. But I saw them and I think everyone sees their loved ones in caskets when you're that scared. God, I was scared and part of me didn't want my sister to say anything. Sometimes it's easier not knowing, you know? You can stay up in your head and not deal with reality. God, I hate reality sometimes. 'Mom had a heart attack.' That's what she said. My mom had a heart attack. A heart attack. It sounds so weird when I say it out loud. I don't think I said it out loud. No. I never said it out loud until now. Right now I'm saying it. My mom had a heart attack! God, I don't know how she's going to make all those lifestyle changes. She has to change. She has to change the way she eats or she's going to have to start exercising. Doesn't she have to start exercising? She's in her sixties. I don't think I've ever seen my mom exercise. She doesn't exercise and she loves eating sweets. When I visit, she always has a sweet in her hand or one hanging from her mouth. Jelly beans, doughnuts, any candy, she just loves sweets....and those little Easter peeps...yeah, she loves the peeps. I mean, if you looked up sweets in the dictionary you might see a picture of my mom. My mom, the sweet eater. Now it's fruits and vegetables. Right? Fruits and vegetables. She likes cantaloupes. Cantaloupes are sweet. She ate lots of cantaloupes when we were growing up. One day she shoved two cantaloupes under her shirt and started dancing around the kitchen. She just did it. I don't know why she did it, but I always remember her doing the cantaloupe dance.....I always tell the cantaloupe story to all my friends. So far, I've never met anyone who had a mother who did the cantaloupe dance. An original dance. Maybe it will catch on. The cantaloupe dance. Cantaloupe. Yeah, she can eat cantaloupes again. I'll stop and pick her up some cantaloupes so she'll have some at home when she's discharged. Maybe she'll do the cantaloupe dance for me again if I ask her. You should see her do the cantaloupe dance, Doc. It's pretty funny. I like cantaloupe. Do you like cantaloupe, Doc? *(Beat)* Look how good she looks. Don't you think she looks good for just having a heart attack? She had a heart attack and look how she looks. Amazing. *(Beat)* I'm hungry. I wonder if the cafeteria is serving cantaloupe today....cantaloupe, yes. Cantaloupe sounds good.

From "PEELING"

By Kaite O'Reilly, Irish - Wales, UK

BEATY is disabled, a beautiful young woman of 24

SHE has a reduced life expectancy and has just buried her mother.

BEATY: *(as her Mother)* "You have to entice; you have to beguile. Put it all in the shop window Beatrice, though God knows you have little enough. Put yourself on special offer, dear."

Mothers...who'd be one, eh? They love to maim. But they think it's for our own good. Tough love. They're trying to help because we don't want to get too big for our boots, do we? Mustn't aspire for other things... We have to be kept in our places.

(as her Mother) "Keep your aim low and you'll never be disappointed...You have a short shelf life, Beatrice, though you'd never know by looking at you. So keep smiling dear, and remember, it's quality of life, not quantity."

When they buried her, I had the greatest temptation to laugh down into that hole they were putting her in: "So who was it survived the longest, then?"

She was convinced she'd see me out. Had no idea she was going. But I knew. To the tick. It's a talent I have—I've been thoroughly trained in it—to sense time passing and my old mate, the grim reaper, stalking close behind. All my life, thanks to my mum, I've felt the tip of his scythe touching the nape of my neck. My mother was so focused on that, waiting for me to croak, she didn't notice the big fingers come to snuff her out.

So I buried her.

There's not many with "reduced life expectancy" can say that. It's an achievement. There's not many like me can press the earth down on their mother's face. Stamp on the grave. Put a layer of concrete over so she can't rise again.

I joke of course.

Though she was the joker in our family.

She'd call me into the bathroom and make me stare at her face. She was getting deep crow's feet around her eyes—she hated it—and the skin around her jaw line was beginning to soften—sag a bit—her face covered in fine hairs, like the fur of a peach. And she'd cradle her face in her hands and stretch back the skin so the wrinkles would disappear and she'd say "That's what I looked like when I was 16. You're lucky, Beatrice. Just think, you'll never have lines on your face like me— you'll never see your features blurring, you'll never suffer from the ravages of age. You're so lucky, Beatrice. You're so lucky you'll die when you're young. You're so lucky you'll never live to be old."

CHLORINE ECLIPSE

From "Tophet Point"

By Chris Shaw Swanson, USA

SARA, 20s-30s is questioning pregnancy

SARA questions her ability to be a good mother and ponders the likelihood of becoming pregnant.

SARA: *(To audience)* And where do I get off allowing myself to play infertility treatment roulette? What if I suck at motherhood? *(Pause)* In my girlhood day, all the married neighbor ladies had kids. I wonder if they analyzed and agonized over their maternal instinct—or just let her rip!

We were modern Mattel moms, my best friend Suzie and me. I had one Barbie and Suzie had one Barbie and one Ken and all of the couple's relatives, friends, and plastic accessories. We were playing Barbies in my backyard and this cloud...this translucent yellow cloud suddenly swept through the trees and engulfed us. At last, Suzie and I were experiencing our first eclipse—and boy, did it stink! We closed our eyes real tight to prevent going blind, although we knew we'd seen enough of it already that at least we'd need prescription glasses. Then my mother was running out of the back door in her torn housecoat, yelling at us to jump on our bikes and ride somewhere...Where? Just anywhere, she screamed. So we did. Suzie and I rode anywhere. We rode like hell. And neither Suzie nor I nor the other five girls on the block have been able to get pregnant. A chlorine gas leak from the sewage plant down the road. My crack infertility doctor says seven girls, it's a coincidence, there's no data, no proof that chlorine causes later-life infertility...It certainly hasn't hurt Barbie—look how she's multiplied!

(With difficulty) So Suzie and I, we stroll along, nauseated every time we smell the yellow stench of chlorine, of our...eclipse, while our vision of the all-American family, the all-American dream, slowly blurs and fades...and fades...

IT'S YOUR BODY

By Elizabeth Whitney, USA

FEMALE, mid-20s, speaking about birth control

FEMALE: Robby Lenitz was bad, really bad, and he was only in third grade. He taught all of us neighborhood kids a really nasty song about a guy who met a girl on a train and they went home and did it. It had this sing-songy rhythm to it that was really catchy:

"Doody-wop, I met this dame, doodywop, her name was Jane, doodywop..."

He asked me to marry him. Actually he asked me if I wanted to do it with him, just like the people on the train, but I guess we figured that since you have to be married to do it, we should get married. He wrote me a note asking me to do it, which my mother found. She sighed and looked at me, hard, and said, "well, it's your body." I was in fifth grade.

We had a mock wedding in my driveway. The other neighborhood kids were attendants, flower girls, some of them threw things that were supposed to be rice, and then Anthony Schecht from four houses down pronounced us married. I wore a makeshift veil. I was so nervous, processing down the driveway toward Robby, trying not to trip on broken cement that was busting out at crazy angles from the tree roots underneath. We kissed to make it official, just barely touching lips, but we never did get around to doing it, or anything close.

When I was in high school and more seriously considering doing it with my boyfriend, I went to Planned Parenthood and started taking birth control. My mother found that note, too. I guess I wasn't ever too great at hiding things. Well, it's my body. *Doodywop.*

HANNAH CARMEN JACOBS

From "sky too big"

By Karen Jeynes, South Africa

SARA, a twenty something white South African woman

SHE is married to Zane, a coloured man, and pregnant. SHE is a writer by profession.

SARA: So Hannah Carmen Jacobs was born, weighing 4.2kgs and measuring 52cm, after twenty-two hours of labour. The Hannah's for my grandmother, Hannetjie, and the Carmen's from Zane's favourite opera and we're not just saying that to sound cultured. After just 2 weeks she's gained point 8 of a kg and 2cm. *(SHE smiles vacantly)* How am I? Oh fine, fine...you can tell I'm lying can't you? I am not fucking fine. She never sleeps for more than twenty minutes at a time. So just when I've made the cup of tea, rooibos tea, because did I mention I can't drink caffeine, alcohol or anything with citric acid, because citric acid gives her a rash, just when I've sat down with my cup of tea and switched the tv on - I've started watching Ricki Lake, I'm that desperate for stimulation beyond goo goo ga ga - she starts niggling. And I try to ignore it, but she just gets louder and louder...And often, often she wakes up if I even tried to put her down, so I end up going to the loo holding baby, getting dressed holding baby...and I just kept thinking why did nobody warn me? And I haven't even mentioned my leaky, lumpy boobs that no longer feel like part of my body! And then, I thought, ok, ok, I've got post natal depression, I can take medication, but they told me no, I'm normal! That this is bloody normal! They say "Don't worry love, you'll settle down, you'll be fine." Do I look FINE to you?

BATTLEGROUND

From "sky too big"

By Karen Jeynes, South Africa

SARA, a twenty something white South African woman.

Lights come up on SARA, who is surrounded by boxes, clothes, etc. SHE moves about picking up clothes, folding them and putting them in boxes. SHE is talking on the cellphone.

SARA: It's fucking fantastic! We're moving house, I'm 8 and a half months pregnant and trying to get a huge article in on deadline and ma "wants to talk." Like I haven't heard it all before. "Are you sure you should quit your job?"—"Why don't you come and stay, just while baby's little?"—"What are you planning to name the baby?" I don't know why she wants to talk to me, my mother is perfectly capable of having a conversation all on her own. She asks the questions and of course she has the answers!

(SARA clears a chair and collapses with a sigh of relief.)

There's only two times I remember ma being speechless. The day I brought Zane home, and the day we moved here. That's what really pisses me off you know, she goes on about being all liberal with her feminist ideals and all that but really she's a stuck up snob! "You're moving where, darling? Observatory? I don't think I've ever been to Observatory..." So I told her it's easy to find, all you do is you drive along Main Rd towards town, and when you smell the zol...the weed...the dagga? Ja, you turn right. "But darling, it's not safe there, it's full of layabouts and drug addicts!" "So was University, ma, and you made me go there for four years!" I wasn't all that excited about moving to Observatory myself, but if it's a choice between my ma and drug addicts, I'll take the drug addicts any day of the week! Oh, Jess, I must go I've got another call, I'll speak to you later, bye!

Hello love! You'll never guess who just phoned. My bloody mother! Mmmm...so anyway she did her usual mind control tactics and I agreed to go around for supper tonight. Mmm...oh god no! Can't you miss practice just once? Well can you come around straight after and rescue me? Ok. Ok. I'll see you around nine then? Please don't be late, you know what she's like, by the time you come I'll probably have agreed to name the baby after my great aunt...Love you too. Bye!

(SHE puts the phone down and sinks once again into the chair. SHE breathes deeply, then picks up the cellphone and dials again.)

Jess? Where was I? No, God, ma doesn't even know we're moving yet, she'll be thrilled to have us out of the slums of Observatory! Probably less thrilled when she hears that we're moving to Goodwood. The Northern Suburbs. No Jess, you don't understand, ma is very proud of having risen above her rural background to take her place in the Southern Suburbs, and treats people from the Northern Suburbs, the Wrong Side of the Railway, like people with half a brain! You wouldn't think she would be prejudiced against people who speak less than perfect English, but she is. The thing is, we can afford Goodwood, you know, and it's really nice out there, none of these high walls and security guards. I often feel like I'm entering enemy territory when I go to my parents, security vans patrolling, barbed wire and cut glass, sirens going off as soon as they see Zane approaching. That's not how I like it, I like to know my neighbours, I like them to know me. Here it's great, you know, there's a real sense of community. Everyone can tell you who stole your car radio, or your letterbox! "Yes, it was that Naicker boy, you know that short one that looks like a chimp. I saw him hanging around here all afternoon, man you should complain to his parents you know last week he stole old Mrs Snyman - yes that old lady with the purple hair - he stole her radio right out of her kitchen while she was in the front watching tv. I saw him with my own eyes!" Oooh. I think I must go lie down, I need to gather strength for tonight. Ok Jess. Sorry for ranting at you. See you tomorrow!

From "HURRICANE IN A GLASS"

By Kimberly del Busto, Cuban-American, USA

DOLORES, in her 20s, of Cuban heritage

DOLORES: I was going to tell you...When I got back. Mom, it's different for me. You and *Abuela,* you know where you are from. But what about me? What am I? A Cuban name. A Cuban girl, never having been to the island. There is a country in Miami that I don't know. You all are always saying to me: "This street is named after one in Cuba," "This restaurant is a recreation of a place in *la habana vieja....*" You can say that because you were there. I know Cuba only from your memories. From words. Not even from many pictures, because I haven't been able to see much of anything. So when I saw the "Teaching & Touring for Peace" program, where I could work in Cuban education systems while learning something myself—I applied. No, it's not like that. It is completely ethical travel. Politically neutral. I will do the teaching. So what, it's only English grammar, "I walk, you walk, he walks..."! And to experience the island—my family's home—I'd go along with the tours but remain for the most part independent, making my own notes, and that's it. I really was going to tell you—once I returned, once you could see that there was nothing to it. And *Abuela* said that if you knew, you would have a breakdown while I was there, and she was right, because look at you now and I'm not even gone. Mom, calm—*Abuela,* tell her...Mom, she knew, I swear. She helped me with the paperwork. I had her permission.

PAGAN BABE

From "Chalk Temple"

By Isabella Russell-Ides, USA

The PAGAN BABE is a world mix, young & lovely

A cosmological monologue.

PAGAN BABE: *(Enters, wearing band aides & bandages & book pages stuck to her clothing, or perhaps an astonishing cape made of book pages: SHE is a pretty punk/monk, a prophetess, the world's waif.)*

Welcome to the spring—rice pagan fling. Or is it summer? It seems summer is always pressing on us these days. It comes in waves. Tsunamis of heat. I've lost all sense of season. Come to this. These times. This place. Welcome to the Chalk Temple. This play. This prison. This season of dust. Am I forgetting something? Oh yes. Please—turn off all cell phones and pagers. Has someone already been here? Stood here? Said this? There have been budget cuts and surgeries. Brain cells have died of thirst. Artists starved in garrets. Dried up like raisins. New deserts have been born. Blooms of dust. Seas of sand. And there have been great gatherings of water in other places. Lack here. Abundance there. That is the way of it. Cities and peoples washed away. Washed away I tell you. And arks appeared everywhere in the satellite photographs. But here we are, snug in the nowhere. One bucket of water. One cup of rice. Enough. Enough for the prisoners. Enough for the Monks.

There is a story told about how Tibetan Monks taken prisoner will sometimes redraw their temples in chalk on the floors and the walls of the prison. This is not that story. We are under a more strictly ruled regime. Here we must erase all evidence of art by day-break to avoid reprisals. However, there have been budget cuts and I am not certain the guards will come again. No one is. Uncertainty is one of the charms of this place. That and the budget cuts. You see how cut up I am. Cut up but not cut. We lost the forth Monk. Gone. There was a mountain of rice, I tell you. Right there, down stage left. You see—how the space is filled with nothing! Take a closer look. There it is—the ghost of a rice mountain. Oh, the fourth Monk was a wonder! A wonder I tell you. *(Tibetan flute sonata fades in. PAGAN BABE mimes the fourth Monk's movements)* With a small feather he would pick up one grain of rice. How reverently he would carry this one grain of precious rice to the prayer cloth. Just as I have done. Well no, not quite. In truth I cannot compare. The fourth Monk could walk on air and would float to the floor like a dropped handkerchief. And the rice would tumble each time to its perfect place on the prayer cloth. You see, here is the rice pile. One cup. How perfect it is. That much remains of the fourth Monk. Prosaic, yes—this miniature mountain. But he could feed millions with this one cup, make a meal with one grain and divide it up. Serve leftovers, the next day. He also gave us a prophecy about a girl but she never comes. And he gave me a pomegranate but I've long since eaten it.

Still, we are not without our miracles here. Chalk Talk. Cave drawings. Oh, the Monks have outdone themselves tonight. But soon it must all be erased. Sponges. Buckets. Budget cuts. What a misfortune it should always end like this. Each night after we turn off the cell phones and dim the lights, I let myself hope again that the play will come out differently. Sometimes as the Monks move through their paces, I become an aerial and pick up atavistic signals in my cells. I remember things. In the beginning there was a word, a rumor spread through the angel herd—a rumor of creation! One of the planets has come alive, the heralds cried! There are fires in the caves! And hope stampeded the angel herd, coursed through us all like an electrical current. It was word. Then, the sounding of millions of wings pounding. My heart races even telling it. By the time we arrived, there were already holes in the atmosphere. I can hear my mother's voice calling me back, "stay away from the edge!" Too late. The herd surged and I fell. You see how cut up I am. And no money for repairs. All the money has gone into the Great War. There is always a Great War. We've stopped numbering them. And price of gasoline, how it soars! Even the monks hesitate at the cost of self-immolation. Frankly, no one knows what is going on. The guards seem to have abandoned their posts. But we can't leave the prison. We are still waiting for the girl who never comes. I probably should not have eaten the pomegranate. Perhaps it was meant for her. Although at the time, it was a temptation too much. Now I am full of seed and fed for eternity. I am pages from books, the sides from a play, these words incarnate. Separated from my mother and my name. I have no name. Check the program. See for yourself. I am the girl who never arrives. I am the Lost Bride—*(Rips off one of the book pages that is stuck to her costume)* foreign, orphaned, oracular *(Reads, a paraphrase of William Blake)*—the mate and companion of people, all of them just as immortal and fathomless as myself: affectionate, haughty, electrical and I, this mystery in a Temple gone to chalk dust and from dust each morning newly risen. Did the master not say—take a hard look around when the long rain begins to fall? See who remains. And here I am. I am the motherless remainder. I carry the seeds of the future within. I have heard the far off rumbles of the great rain coming. And voice of the master in my ear—he says, mark well each one who boards your ark when the waters rise in the final days. New gods will fall in among you. Welcome them!

SEVENTEEN TIARAS

From "Adeste Infidelis"

By Isabella Russell-Ides, USA

MELONY is a young southern beauty

SHE is whimsical, naive, caught at a turning point. This piece is a delicate, sometimes humorous, often quirky examination of one girl's American dream gone awry.

MELONY: I want to take you home and meet my mother. Celestine. She'd think you were the most gorgeous thing. She'd want to put you in a glass case. He's a keeper, that's what Celestine would say. Of course, she'd get all the wrong ideas. And start pestering me about my naked ring finger. No. No. No, sweetie. I'm not complaining. I love the diamond bracelet. You know how I am when I'm nervous. I just blurt things out. No. I did not tell her. I am not a home-wrecker. I am not. I want things to work for you and Emily. Really. I promise. I never said a word. She knew everything. She knew about the Bahamas, the diamond tennis bracelet and putting the chocolate bonbons up my vagina. Your wife—she's like god. I'm afraid of her Harold. Oh honey, I'm sorry. What a mess.

I wish we could drive to Georgia. Georgia's like that band aide that makes everything feel better. You could see my tiara collection. My mother keeps all my tiaras in a special glass case. Seventeen tiaras. Each one sits on its own velvet cushion. Miss Sweet Potato. Miss Georgia Peach. And there's one made entirely of red Jalapeño Peppers from when I moved here and was Bean Queen in the Miss Texas Chile cook-off competition—that was right before I met you. Remember? I put it in my resume.

I won my first tiara when I was just seven years old—in a Tiny Twirlers pageant. I walked down that ramp and my feet never touched the floor. I floated like an angel in little silver slippers—the closest

I've ever come to heaven. No little girl ever dreams, when she grows up, she's going to be the other women. I don't guess little boys dream they're going to grow up and be cheaters. I wish we could jump the clock backwards and my seven-year-old could date your seven-year-old self. If I were God, there'd be a place like that—where none of this had ever happened yet.

No, I'm not trying to make you feel worse. Please, don't – don't go. *(Watches him leave, then to herself.)* Bye. Harold.

I've always been a fool. Easily fooled. Played the fool. My mother told me the only reason for a pretty woman to have a man was to keep all the other ones from bothering you. But I'm not like her. I fall in love. I love Harold. Harold loves Emily. I used to fantasize about her death: a plane crash or a car wreck or a slow wasting disease, like leukemia. And I would be there to comfort Harold. Steady as a rock. Or, sometimes and this was my favorite—I'd pretend that I was Marilyn Monroe and she was Jackie Kennedy and Harold, of course, would be the President of the United States of America. *(Sings)* Happy Birthday Mr. President. Then I'd be the one to comfort Jackie, when Harold got shot in the parade—in Dallas. And here's the best part—in the fantasy—Jackie and I turn out to be best girlfriends. I can picture it in my mind, clear as cellophane. The two of us open a jewelry boutique, "The Pink Lady"—and specialize in tiaras. Jackie's tiara, the one from the Inaugural Ball, is the major attraction. And of course, my seventeen tiaras are on display as well. Side-by-side Tiaras. The other day I was riding around in my car, listening to the sound track from Thelma and Louise. I love that old movie. Then I saw us, me and Jackie, driving off the cliff into the big nowhere. And Harold beside himself with grief at our funeral. Weeping his little eyes out. But I don't know. Sometimes I wonder—what if there is no big daddy in the sky, with his arms open as wide as heaven to catch your turquoise Thunderbird when it tumbles into eternity? What if you just fall forever? And Harold just goes off and finds himself another girl.

(Taking off the diamond bracelet) I miss my mother. But, this isn't the kind of story a girl wants to bring home. On the other hand, I know

Celestine like I know my own heart. *(Bracelet held up in the palm of her hand)* And—she is going to love this bracelet.

IMPACT

By Margaret Bail, USA

A 20-something SINGLE MOTHER

SETTING: Woman standing on an empty stage with a shopping bag at her feet.

SINGLE MOTHER: When my daughter was born, I was determined that I wouldn't raise her as a prissy little girly girl. I wasn't going to dress her in pink ruffly dresses or only let her play with "girl toys" like Barbies or Easy Bake Ovens. I wanted her to have choices, even as a little girl. I wanted her to understand that she really can be anything she wants to be, and that being a woman isn't a handicap.

And so far, I think I've done a pretty good job of sticking with that plan. I mean, sure she's only four years old, but she doesn't wear pink. She doesn't even own a dress. Well, okay just one dress, but my mom gave it to her for her birthday last year. And I know for sure she's never worn it.

I just want her to be an independent woman. I want her to understand that my expectations are only that she try her best at whatever she does. I don't want her to succumb to the pressure to play with toy kitchens and vacuum cleaners if what she really wants is to play with Hot Wheels and Army Men.

(pause)

It turns out that raising a daughter is a lot harder than I thought it would be. And here I thought being a woman and raising a woman would be a piece of cake.

(pause - pulls frilly pink dolly out of shopping bag)

But . . .I saw this at the store today.

And for some reason, I felt compelled to buy it for her. I don't understand why. It's like some evil mother twin took over my body. I saw her reaching for the doll and I felt trapped in my own head watching, screaming at her to "drop the doll!" but I had no control of over her and she bought it anyway.

(pause)

It's just so cute I couldn't help myself. Its got such pretty hair, and cute little baby toes, and it comes with 3 different outfits.

(pause)

So now what do I do? If I give her the doll am I caving in to conformist pressure to raise a girly girl? Will I be a failure as a mother?

Will giving her this doll mean she'll be a nurse instead of a doctor? A secretary instead of an executive? A housewife instead an astronaut, or president of the United States?

Can one doll really have that much impact?

I mean, I played with dolls when I was a girl. I loved playing house with my sisters. We played school, and we played with Barbies, and we played dress up. And I turned out okay.

My mom never told me I could be anything I wanted to be when I grew up. The only thing she ever did was to encourage me to find a nice man while I was in college. Which I did. "Be sure you marry well," was the best advice she had to offer. Which I didn't.

I don't want my daughter to be crushed by the weight of my expectations. I don't want her to resent me like I resent my mother. But it's my job to guide her, isn't it? There's got to be a balance between guidance and oppression.

If I can overcome my mother's domestic dreams for me, maybe my daughter can overcome one doll.

How can one baby doll cause so much feminist angst?

If I can't figure this out, what am I going to do when she's a teenager? Am I really cut out to be a mom if I can't even decide whether or not to give her a stupid doll?

I love my daughter more than anything. All I want is what's best for her. To protect her from all the bad stuff in the world. That's no different from any other mother in the world, right?

I just need to lighten up. One doll isn't going to ruin her life. One doll isn't going to have that much influence. One doll can't change what kind of person she is.

(pause - takes a deep breath)

Okay. So, I'll just give her the doll.

(pause - pulls another doll out of shopping bag)

So, if one doll is okay, how bad can two be?...

HAPPY HOLIDAYS FROM ANDERSON, DAVIS, SETON, AND FENNER

By James Venhaus, USA

JULIA, a receptionist at a law firm

Setting: The reception desk in the lobby of a law firm
Time: 4:50 p.m. on December 23rd.

*NOTE: Production rights to **"Happy Holidays from Anderson, Davis, Seton and Fenner"** are controlled by Original Works Publishing. For permission to perform this piece and royalty information, please visit their website at:* www.originalworksonline.com

(At rise we hear a phone ringing and the lights come up on empty reception desk in the lobby of the law firm of Anderson, Davis, Seton and Fenner. A clock on the wall reads 4:55 p.m. Enter JULIA smartly dressed in business attire and wearing a telephone headset with the cord dangling behind her. SHE is straightening her dress and adjusting her hose.)

JULIA: Crap, crap, crap, crap.

(SHE runs behind the desk and plugs her headset cord in)

Happy Holidays from Anderson, Davis, Seton and Fenner. How may I direct your call? Ms. Davis has gone for the day. Would you like her voice-mail?...I'm sorry sir; I can't give you that information. I can put you through to her voice mail. Sir, I just can't give you that number, Ms. Davis left strict *(the caller hangs up)* Hello? Hello? Jerk.

(SHE unplugs the headset and starts to exit and is almost off-stage when the phone rings. SHE lets out an exasperated sigh as SHE runs back behind the desk)

Happy Holidays from Anderson, Davis,...Oh, Hi Amanda....It has been so slow. Almost everyone is gone for the holidays, and there hasn't been a soul walk through the front door in almost three hours. But it seems like every time I try to do anything or go to the bathroom...*(another line starts to ring)* Oh, hang on a sec. Happy Holidays from Anderson, Davis, Seton and Fenner. How may I direct your call? Thank you and have a nice day...Are you still there Amanda? Actually, can I call you right back. I had just stepped out to the ladies room when you called...Thanks.

(SHE hangs up, unplugs the headset and exits. After a beat, the phone rings.)

Are you kidding me?

(SHE runs behind the desk and plugs her headset cord in)

Happy Holidays from Anderson, Davis, Seton and Fenner. How may I...Amanda, that is not funny. I had just made in to the bathroom and...Of course, I was running...Stop laughing. I don't think this is very...I'm hanging up now.

(SHE hangs up, stares at the phone for a beat, then unplugs the headset and barely makes it from behind the desk when the phone rings. SHE mumbles something under her breath and plugs the headset back in)

Listen Amanda, CUT IT OUT. I don't appreciate being...Oh, hello Mr. Anderson...No sir, not at all. No, that's not how I...I've been saying Happy Holidays from Ander—...I'm sorry sir, I thought you were someone else...Yes sir. It won't happen again.

(SHE hangs up and before SHE can do anything, the phone rings)

Happy Holidays from Anderson...Amanda, I could kill you. That was my boss on the other line. I almost bit his head off...Well, he sounded confused but I could tell he was not happy...No I can't tonight. I've got to be a Macy's at 5:30, and after that Chris and I are going out...Yeah, tonight's the big night. I'm kind of nervous. I think he might say those three little words that I've...*(the phone rings)* gotta go. Call me back.

Happy Holidays from Anderson, Davis, Seton and Fenner. How may I direct your call? Oh Chris, I'm glad you called. Listen, I get off in a few minutes and...What?!...Not again. Chris don't. Please...You've cancelled twice already...Cancel, reschedule, whatever. You know what I...Alright, when?...I guess so. No, it's OK, I understand. *(The phone rings)* I gotta go, call me back *(SHE hangs up and answers the other line)*

Happy Holidays from Ander—...Hey, Amanda. Do you still want to go to the movies tonight?...Yes, can you believe it? Not only that, but he calls five minutes before I get off work...He said he had to work late, and I know that he...No, I don't think he would. Would he?...I mean, if there was someone else, I could tell (beat) couldn't I? (the phone rings) I'll call you back.

(SHE hangs up and answers the other line)

Happy Holidays from Anderson, Davis, Seton and Fenner. How may...Oh, hi Mom...I can't...No, Mom...We've had this conversation before. I have to work. No, the firm is closed, but I'll be at Macy's until Christmas Eve...Well, I needed the money and it pays well. Plus, I get a discount...In the, um, children's department. Look, I know it's been a while since I've visited, but...Well, you can mail them to me, I guess, or I can pick them when I come down next month...No, mother, this is not because of him. I'm not sure that we are even still...Mom, please don't cry. *(the phone rings)* Mom, hold on, I've got to...Mom, calm down. I have to answer the other line.

(SHE puts MOTHER on hold and answers the other line)

Happy Hol—...Oh my God, Amanda. You wouldn't believe what just happened. I told my mother that I'm not coming home for Christmas, and she just started freaking out. Crying and saying that we never spend time together and that the holidays are so important in the twilight of her years, and blah, blah, blah. She's fifty-two for God's sake. She's nuts...*(shocked)* I don't know. If so, she hasn't told me. She'd tell me if she was sick or something, wouldn't she? Wouldn't she? Holy cow, I've left her on hold. Hang on one sec.

(SHE puts Amanda on hold picks up the other line)

Mom, don't worry. I'll be there. I'll drive down after I get off from Macy's. It'll be late, so keep some dinner warm...I love you too. *(phone rings)* I gotta go.

(SHE hangs up and answers the other line)

Happy Holidays from Anderson, Davis, Seton and Fenner. How may I...No, Ms. Davis is...Sir, I still can't give out that kind of information. It's against *(the caller hangs up)* Asshole!

(SHE picks up AMANDA'S line)

Hey Amanda, thanks for being so...*(SHE looks back at the clock)* Oh my God, it's almost five. I'm supposed to be gone already and I haven't even changed. The phone has been ringing off the hook all of a sudden and I haven't had a chance to *(the phone rings)* Argh! Hold on.

(SHE puts Amanda on hold and runs over to a coat rack and gets down a hanging bag. SHE unzips it and takes out an elf costume. SHE takes the costume looks at the phone, then at the costume, then back at the phone again. SHE looks around to make sure no one is looking, and takes the costume behind the desk with her)

Happy Holidays from Anderson, Davis, Seton and Fenner. How may I direct your call. *(As SHE speaks, SHE starts changing clothes behind the desk)* Hello again, Mr. Anderson...No sir, I can't...I thought the office was closed on Christmas Eve...Oh, I see...I'm sorry sir I just can't...If you don't mind me saying sir, I don't feel that is fair. I asked off for this day months ago and...I know that sir, and I wish I could help you out, but...How much?...I could use the overtime. What the heck. I'll do it. See you tomorrow. Goodbye, sir.

(SHE hangs up and answers the other line)

Happy Holidays from Anderson, Davis, Seton and Fenner. How may I direct...Chris. *(beat)* Hi...Listen, I was talking to Amanda just now and I was wondering: Is there anybody *(SHE can't bring herself to finish)* never mind. What were you going to say?...I'd love to, but I just promised my boss that I'd work that day, then I told my Mom I would drive down...Excuse me?...Well, I don't think you've got any right to...This is not my fault, you're the one that cancelled...But, I only made those plans after you...*(the phone rings)* Listen, I gotta go. Call me when you—on second thought, don't bother!

(SHE hangs up and is almost completely changed into her elf costume. SHE lets the phone ring a few times while SHE finishes changing clothes)

Happy Holidays from Anderson, Davis, Seton and Fenner. How may I direct your call? *(SHE strains to hear the caller)* I'm sorry sir. I can't hear you very well. It sounds like your cell phone...I said it sounds like your cell...I'm sorry sir, you're what? On your way where?...Oh my!...Oh no, nothing's wrong, it's just that...I'm supposed to be gone already, but, I'll have that ready for you when you get here...You're welcome sir. I'll see you in a few minutes.

(SHE hangs up and takes AMANDA off of hold)

Amanda, I'm going to have to call you back. My boss will be here in a few minutes, and I look like an elf on crack and I have to prepare this *(SHE holds up the file and all of the papers fall onto the floor)* Crap. I just dropped all of the...Dammit! I'll call you right back.

(SHE hangs up, forgets to detach her headset, reaches for the papers and SHE reaches the end of the cord and falls backwards behind the desk. The phone rings. SHE lets it rings a few times as SHE tries to compose herself. SHE is almost in tears. There are now multiple lines ringing.)

Happy Holidays from Anderson, Davis, Seton and Fenner, can you hold please? *(SHE places the caller on hold and answers the next line)* Anderson, Davis, Seton and Fenner, can you hold please? *(SHE places the caller on hold and answers the next line)* Anderson and associates can you hold? *(SHE places the caller on hold and answers the next line)* Hold please.

(SHE tosses her headset down and starts to cry. After a moment or two, SHE picks up her headset and begins to put her dress back on over her elf costume.)

Thank you for holding, how may I direct your call?...Sir, I can not give you Ms. Davis' personal...I don't care if you're the freakin' Pope! She doesn't want to be bothered. Now, I'm putting you through to her voice mail, and if your lucky, I'll tell her to check it when I see her. Goodbye and Merry-fucking-Christmas.

(SHE hangs up. The other lines are still ringing as SHE reaches to pick up the other line then changes her mind)

I am not answering this phone because *(SHE disconnects a caller)* we *(SHE disconnects another)* are *(SHE disconnects another)* closed! *(SHE disconnects the last one, takes a moment and opens an outside line, and dials a number)*

Hello Chris, it's me. Do you have minute to talk? Listen, about before: I think we might have both overreacted a bit...I'm sorry, too...Look, I know that you are busy, I'm working two jobs, and we're both stressed out. Maybe we should cut each other some slack...Me, too . . .You know, I know this is a weird time to say it, but, my life has been really crazy lately, and what you and I have is about the only normal thing I've got right now, but - I love you. I know this isn't a very romantic moment, but hear me out. I love you and I want to make this work. I'm willing to commit to that if you are. It means we have to be honest with each other and make time for ourselves and make time to be together. Even if we sacrifice a few things...You do? Me too...Really? Oh, Chris, this feels wonderful. Like we're starting on a whole new *(SHE can't think of the right word)* something. So, what are you doing tomorrow? My schedule just cleared up. I'd love to spend Christmas with you, too. Great...Great. I'll come over early and we can go out for breakfast. I love you too. Bye. Oh Chris. Keep your schedule open for New Years. I've got something special planned for you. *(SHE hangs up and dials another number)*

Hello, Mom. It's me. Listen, I need you to hear me out. When I tell you this, I don't want to hear any of your dramatics. No crying, no guilt trip, just listen. I love you, but I don't want to come home for Christmas...I need this time for me...Mom, this is what I want, and this is what I'm going to do...Look, what are you doing for New Years? I'd love to come and visit. There's someone I want you to meet...Great. I'll see you next week...No, it's OK, I've got a little more time off from work that I thought I would have. I love you too. Bye Mom. *(SHE hangs up and dials another number. During the next conversation, SHE takes off her office dress and is back in her elf costume)*

Hello, Mr. Anderson, it's Julia. Sir, I thought you would be here by now, but...Oh, I see...Anyway, sir, it's after five, and I have to leave now or I'll be late for another engagement. So, I'm going to leave the file you asked for at the front desk. By the way, I won't be able to work tomorrow. In fact, I won't be working for you at all any more...I know this is very short notice, but I've left the number of the temp agency on top of your file...Well sir. It's personal. There are just some other things I need to be doing right now. I'm sorry sir, but I hope you understand. Thank you sir. Merry Christmas to you too. Goodbye.

(SHE hangs up the phone. Places the headset on the desk and starts to exit when the phone rings. Out of instinct, SHE stops and turns back towards the desk. SHE stops, smiles, turns on her heels and exits. The lights dim as the phone continues to ring.)

A BOWL

From "Thing Quartet"

By Mark Harvey Levine, USA

DORINDA, 20s, is a young Latina nanny

DORINDA: This kid. This kid I look after. You walk around the house, there's a one foot layer of toys you have to wade into. It's like a Toys R Us exploded in here. It's crazy. I don't know how she could possibly play with them all. She's only six months old. And already she has more possessions than I've had in my entire life. I miss some of my things. Not my toys, but—It's not that I miss the things, exactly...It's the memories inside them. I store my memories in things.

A spoon. When I was eight my sister Sophia hit me in the head with a spoon so hard I saw little shooting points of light. I started to cry but my mother wasn't there. It was best to cry around my mother because my father wouldn't do anything. But my father came and picked me up and held me and sort of...bounced me up and down. Like I was an infant. I don't think he knew what else to do but he wanted to do...something. And that was the last time he ever picked me up.

I would think about that every time I saw that one spoon—I could tell which one it was, it was bent, Sophia hit me so hard. And I would be happy every time I saw it. I store all my memories in things. Stupid girl! I should store my memories in my head like other people. I had to leave all my things behind. I took one thing only. A bowl. A simple little ceramic bowl. I packed it carefully, putting my few meager clothes around it so it wouldn't break. And I carried it all the way here.

My mother made the bowl. She was very smart, my mother, brilliant with the cello but very bad at pottery. She kept trying to learn, she would take classes, she would practice, but she didn't have the talent for it. But she made this one thing, one bowl only that actually turned out well. And then she handed it to me. "Why are you giving this to me?" I asked. "It's your one perfect bowl! You may never make another!" I was allowed to tease her. Nobody else was. And she said that I was something else perfect, that she had made, and she wanted the two of us to be together.

Wasn't that a nice thing to say to someone? That's a memory I wanted to keep. So I brought the bowl here. I was so honored by what that bowl meant, and I wanted to show it to the lady I work for and tell her the story. So she'd know I wasn't just a nanny. That there was more to me. That I am special, a perfect bowl, filled with good things.

So one day I wrapped it up very carefully so it wouldn't break, and I brought it to show Mrs. Herricks. I held it out to her all ready to tell the story about it, when she started unwrapping it and saying "you shouldn't have...you shouldn't have." I stood there and my whole body felt numb, and I saw those same little points of light like when Sophia hit me with the spoon. She smiled politely, but I could see it didn't even make her happy. And she said "It's lovely" and set it on a shelf with a thousand other little knick-knacks that I end up dusting. Stupid girl. Stupid girl. I shouldn't keep my memories in things.

SMART GIRLS

From "Thing Quartet"

By Mark Harvey Levine, USA

BECCA, 20s-30s, is a young expectant mother, a little high-strung

BECCA: This kid! This girl. Oh my GOD! This girl is driving me crazy! And she's not even born yet! All these...things have been arriving. Presents. Spoons. Bibs. Blankets. Toys. Diapers. Bottles. Socks. Bowls. Things! What am I going to do with all these things?! And I still don't even believe I'm going to be a mother. It's all an elaborate hoax. To get people to go to Toys R Us and buy us things. Don't get me wrong. I'm very happy about it. We're both very happy. Happyhappyhappy! And a little stunned. Worried. When the doctor told me I was pregnant, I got light-headed and saw stars! It's like I saw her whole life pass before my eyes. I saw her grow up! And she was a nice person. Very smart! A very smart girl! Played the viola. My mother says the same thing happened when she found out she was having me. Of course, we have a talent for hysterics in my family. Handed down from one hysterical woman to the next. They tease me about it at work. They jump out from around corners just to hear me scream. It's really not nice. But I mean, I want this girl to be...I don't know...Smart. Funny. Special. And I shouldn't feel guilty for wanting my daughter to be...I don't know...I want her to be happy, sure, but- A thousand other things, too. But mostly—Smart. A smart girl. A smart girl. The thing is...Smart girls usually aren't happy.

From "NEW YORK'S FINEST"

By Martha Patterson, USA

FIONA, A secretary, 28 years old

SHE is frustrated and angry at the quality of her life in New York City.

FIONA: Yeah, sure, Mom, I could live in New York City in a drunken stupor the rest of my days wearing no make-up and looking like my evil twin. Oh, God, you're right. I'm SO MUCH better off alone. I can dwell alone in my own private hell, ranting and raving about the stupid, fucked-up things people do every day in this city that drive me crazy. Like letting this homeless woman live alone out on Broadway under the bushes of the median strip. She lies on the hoods of cars parked on the street, pissing on herself, stinking of urine, and she LIVES UNDER THE BUSHES ON THE MEDIAN STRIP. Really lovely. Or I could think about the countless panhandlers who shove their paper cups under my nose every day when I pass the bank downstairs, because they need a fucking quarter to help them buy some coffee or a shot of booze somewhere. Or I could think about the five times I've had my bag ripped off my shoulder on the street down in the Village or had my pocket picked at Penn Station while I was on the way home for Christmas, after, AFTER, mind you, I had just cashed my paycheck and had about 350 dollars on me so there was NO WAY they weren't gonna make good on the deal. Oh, fuck, they probably needed the money more than I did, right? And then I could dwell on the subject of Derek, who left me for some bimbo who probably had her shit more together than I do, that is, she probably had more money and a better job and didn't swear so much. SHE probably made him happy. You're so damned right, Mom. I'm SO MUCH better off alone.

IN MY MOTHER'S HOUSE

By Meg Haley, USA

A WOMAN in her mid to late twenties

SHE is a strong, sensitive woman who understands that coming into her own means both embracing and redefining the things held dear and taught by her mother.

WOMAN: In my mother's house, it is cold in the basement where I sleep on an air mattress that could fit inside my great grandmother's bed frame that still resides in this room.

But I don't.

I still have a closet of clothes I'm either waiting to come back into fashion or until I lose weight again or they're only sweaters I'd wear to family functions anyway.

There is a dressing table like my mother's that I always imagined would have lace spread across it and would hold perfume and secrets like hers does still. Instead it holds high school memories. My perfume and secrets don't live here anymore.

In my mother's house there are dreams and memories and memories of dreams I had not so long ago. I still have some—similar—really not that different at all. To me.

But to her, in her house, they've changed drastically, those dreams that are similar. She strives to see the likeness. As long as these dreams become realities enough to make me happy, but stay out of her house, I think she will be fine.

In my mother's house, there are many hors d'oeuvres, wine by the case, and dinner in the oven. Berries for breakfast, and, in honor of a tradition started by her mother, an eggdish. Always, on Christmas morning at my mother's house. I put the angel on the top of the tree with the old kitchen tongs.

In my mother's house, happiness and love are important—like wine and food and presents or cards that cause tears to well.

In my mother's house dreams come true or are cried and hugged away if they cannot. In my mother's house, this Christmas, I will bring a woman to eat, drink and watch as I put the angel on the tree. It will be something like the dreams I used to have, under my mother's roof. I hope she sees the similarity.

From "CLARY'S EXODUS"

By Rachel Rubin Ladutke, USA

CLARICE (CLARY) HAYES: 28. A popular blues singer, known as The Duchess

Staged Reading, William Paterson University, Wayne, NJ: October 2004 Staged Reading, Comedy Alley, Richmond, VA: November 2003

Staged Reading, Villagers Theatre, Somerset, NJ: February 2002 Honorable Mention, Jane Chambers Playwriting Competition

Staged reading of excerpts, Winningstad Theatre, Portland, OR: September 2001

Staged reading, Flatiron Playhouse, New York, NY: August 2001

SETTING: New York City, 1926. Prohibition is in full swing and Harlem nightclubs are sizzling hot. CLARY HAYES, a fast-living black blues singer, shocks her devout Baptist mother with the revelation that her young daughter PHOEBE is half-Jewish. CLARY then secretly enlists the help of ESTHER SOLOMON, a local Rabbi's wife, in teaching Phoebe about her heritage. To everyone's surprise, particularly CLARY's, SHE soon finds herself embarking on her own spiritual journey. And Esther has a secret of her own...

CLARICE: Mama, believe it or not, some things ain't got nothin' to do with you. And some things ain't even your business! Much as you may like them to be! Well, I ain't gonna live my life on your terms, no more. Everything I done since Daddy died was exactly opposite of what you wanted! So I ain't ever done just what I wanted. I done just what you didn't want me to do! Just sometimes it turned out they was the same thing. And who are you to talk, anyways? Your daddy was a preacher man, and you didn't honor him none! You was just as wild as me! You got real religious when you had kids to feed, not before! And you turned right around when you was sixteen and run off with Daddy. Uncle Jones, he told me 'bout all them parties you useta go to, stay out dancin' all night!

Oh, it ain't no sin when you do it, for fun, huh? But when I do it to make a living, it's dirty all of a sudden? That don't make no sense, Mama! And I'll tell you something else, too. You been tryin' all my life to make me a good Christian woman. Well, it ain't never gonna happen. But it ain't because I didn't want to love God. I tried, Mama, so help me. It ain't because Daddy died I stopped goin' to church. It happened 'round the same time, but that was just accidental. Truth is, I was angry. I thought it was my bad thoughts that made God take Daddy away. Then I realized, it wasn't nothin' I done. It was nothin' God done. It was just his time, that's all. Daddy just got sick. But I feared him, your God. I couldn't never love Him 'cause I feared Him too much. And if you'd'a left me alone, maybe I woulda got over it. But no, you couldn't do that. You had to cram it down my throat. And I thought, if He could send you to hell for having bad thoughts, what could I do to stop Him? Not a damn thing. So I might as well have some fun on the way. Then I met Esther, and Rabbi David. Phoebe and I even been to synagogue together, with Esther. And we been learning to pray in Hebrew. A little bit, anyway. And it's finally startin' to make sense to me. We're human, Mama. We're not perfect. We ain't supposed to be perfect. We're supposed to do the best we know how. So it's up to you now, Mama. If this hurts you, I'm sorry. But becoming a Jew, it feels like the right thing for me to do. If you can't stand me doin' this, Phoebe and I can go somewhere else. I ain't sayin' that to threaten you. You can see her anytime you want. I ain't gonna stop you. You're her Nana, and she loves you like crazy. I'm just sayin', I got to do what I got to do, and so do you. So tell me, does it have to be your God or nothing? Or ain't that what matters, really? Finding a way to love God and honor Him? I finally found that way, Mama. You ought to be happy for me. You ought to understand.

SARA

From "...smile...and smile, and be a villain."

By Thomas M. Kelly, Irish - USA

SARA, 29, has an undiagnosed Borderline Personality Disorder

SARA: *(Child crying from the garage)* You want to cry so badly, Elijah, I'll give you something to cry about! *(Laughing.)* You should have heard that fat cop when he stopped me on 285. *(Mimicking the Sheriff's Deputy)* "Now mam, we here in DeKalb County kinda' like ta' keep traffic flowin', but mam you were doin' eighty when ah got behind ya'. Ya'll had ta' be doin' ninety or better 'fore that. Ah'll be needin' your driver's license and registration. Ah'm goin' ta cite ya'll for exceedin' the posted speed limit. Aaahh, ya'll from New York. Ah know for a fact they like ta' drive fast up there. But folks here in DeKalb County respect the law. Ah'll be back in a few minutes. Ya'll just relax. Ah, mam, Ah notice your kids aren't strapped in. No safety belts. Ah'm gonna' cite ya' fer that, too, mam. Now, ya'll just relax there." Ha, Ha, Ha. You were stopped fer speeding. *(Exuberant prolonged laughter)* Ha, Ha, Ha. I gave the cop your driver's license.

I wanted to hurt you as much as you hurt me, bitch. You know how much I need a good attorney. I thought for sure that if I could get you to come down here for Jonah's birthday I could convince you to help me. But, no, you can't take my case. My kids are not as important to you as they are to me. They're your grandkids! You're supposed to be this high-fa-lutin' attorney from New York!

The boys were so upset. Cranky. Crying. They made me so nervous. *(Pause.)* I came back to the neighborhood and parked in the school lot. Just around the corner. *(Beat.)* Jonah kept nagging me. He wanted to play in the school playground. "No, Jonah!" And Elijah, *(Mimicking ELIJAH)* "When are we going home, mommy? I have to pee." "Go behind the car. In a few minutes we'll be going home! I have to think!

I need time to think! I have to make plans! I've got things I have to take care of first." *(Pause.)* While we were on the road it was just a few taps to remind them that I'm the mother. They wouldn't stop whining and crying. I lost it, Mom. They wouldn't stop nagging me. I began hitting them. I slapped Jonah so often and so hard that his face was red. His eyes were swollen. But...*(Slight attempt at nervous laughter...)*...he stopped crying. *(...then remorse.)* I saw the fear, the horror in my baby Elijah' eyes? Then he began sobbing convulsively. I hit him. And I kept hitting him. For no reason. He just sat there with the look of fright...terror in his eyes asking, "Why? Why, Mommy? Why are you doing this to me? I'm just a baby. I'm your baby." Didn't say a word. Didn't cry. He was afraid of me. Me. His mother. They began to cry again. When they wouldn't stop crying, I started whaling on them. But...they just wouldn't stop crying. Screaming. I was beating them for being kids. But they kept it up. I hit them harder. Harder and harder, until they stopped crying. When I looked at them, their eyes were open wide with...terror...helplessness...they were horrified at what I might do next. It was me. Me! They were horrified of ME! I was the monster! *(Pause.)* Your second,...Jerry...He said the same thing to Jimmy and me. You knew what he was capable of. *(Deep male voice)* "You want something to cry about? I'll give you something to cry about." *(Return.)* He was such a coward. And you knew it. He didn't use his hands on me. He used his belt. *(Beat.)* You were no help at all, for fear of getting beaten yourself. Punishment for Jimmy was different. He wanted to show Jimmy how to be a man. He used his fists on Jimmy. Jimmy never recovered. He may not have the swollen face now, but the scars are still there. In prison you get to choose your visitors. He refuses to see you and me. I'm in a prison of my own making.

Now I've lost my babies. Did you see them cowering in fear? Jonah was so afraid of me: his whole body was shaking. He was shaking so much he threw up all over himself. Will my children ever trust me again? Oh, my god. I've lost them. This has to stop.

Is Michael still here? He hasn't left, has he? Oh, my god, I've lost him, too. Another marriage down the tubes. He'll be gone soon, if he's not gone already. He's really a very good man. He loves those boys. What will happen to them now?

Will they live with Edgar? He doesn't want them. He'll just be glad he doesn't have to pay child support. There I go again. I never stop. Edgar loves his sons. He never raised a hand to them. I know he wouldn't. I did though. I can't go on like this. *(SARA reaches into her handbag. SARA puts the gun to her head. Lights out quickly as SARA pulls the trigger.)*

From "TRANSFERENCE"

By Cassandra Lewis, USA

DELANEY MONK, 29, a failed actor

SHE tries to cope with the mental illness that SHE may have inherited from her mother.

DELANEY: For the first time in weeks I took my lunch break only because I was close to tears and blurted out the "F" word after I accidentally hung up on a potential client. The job requires me to be a people person and during the three interviews for the position I believed I was. But the subsequent months of travel and conversations, promoting ideas that seem more like cons than legitimate guarantees, has proven that I have no business near anyone except a bottle of flammable hard liquor. Before Harry, one of the VPs who holds lengthy meetings about the proper way to hold meetings, could loom over my cubicle, I bolted.

The circles under my eyes were so pronounced that I could actually feel the weight of them with each step. It's a similar sensation to wearing earrings that are too heavy. If I had the presence of mind I would have worried that too much walking would stretch out the bags under my eyes and leave me with deep pockets instead of cheeks. Before I got to the edge of the park I saw her. She faced the street and from the back, her over-sized frame, wide shoulders hunched inward—none of this would keep her head low—the homeless woman sat defiantly on two crates with her chin up. It was as though she believed she was guarding the park instead of loitering. In the absurdity and ambiguity of a large woman in the wrong place, I saw my mother.

I stopped suddenly and the suit marching on the path behind me knocked my handbag as he passed. Slowly, I crept towards her. Could it be her? What will I say if it is? Will she attack me? If she does, will this be an adequate excuse to miss the rest of the workday? How can I be so callous at a time like this? When is the appropriate time to be callous? Freud would call this response a defense mechanism, though he would point out it is not the best kind of defense mechanism unless it produces humor. Fuck you, Freud, I thought. Isn't life difficult enough without having to be funny during times of crises?

She must have felt my stare. Before I got in front of her to see her face, she turned her head and looked at me. I gasped. She wasn't my mother, but it had been a while since I'd seen her and I doubted my impression. With the wide eyes of a manner-less child I continued to stare until I passed her. By the time I got to the crosswalk, I realized I was clutching my handbag with both hands. The poor woman must have thought I was afraid she would steal from me or that I was scared of her because she was homeless and not because she was a dead ringer for my mother, who has also been homeless in the past.

Earlier in the kitchen at work I ran into a coworker whom I often avoid because she too reminds me of my mother—not my mother when she was homeless and unpredictable, but the mother I knew when I was seven or younger, the caring mother, full of worrisome advice no one ever wanted to hear.

As I waited to fill my water glass, the coworker described a lobster restaurant on the sea outside of Boston where she was about to visit. I was pretty sure it was the same one my mother used to frequent when she first moved there, before she ran out of money. I nodded knowingly and she asked if I'd ever been to Boston.

"A few times. I used to visit my mother there."

"I have family there too. They just moved so I don't really know my way around yet. Do you have any ideas of places I should visit?"

I thought for a moment and almost mentioned The Pine Street Inn, which is not a quaint bed and breakfast like the name suggests but a homeless shelter. I'm not sure why this place came to mind because I never actually visited my mother there even though she had wanted me to. There must be a place to recommend that could pass as normal, a place where my mother and I exchanged words that weren't accusatory and angry.

"Have you been to Salem yet?" I asked.

"Of the Salem witch trials?"

"That's right. My mother used to live up there too. It's a great place to visit if you need a break from the city."

She moved there shortly after she was eighty-sixed from a major bus route in Boston because she threatened the driver who she believed was "mafia." She was prone to starting fights and Salem's easygoing atmosphere was more conducive to her eccentricities. She spent those years believing she was a witch. In Salem, it was not uncommon to see women in Victorian lace dresses, discussing past lives with sincerity as they wielded wands with moons and stars dangling from the ends.

"It's tragic how women were treated back then and how mental illness was so misunderstood."

"Things haven't changed all that much," I said.

Across the street from the park, fog has blurred the distance between the water and the Bay Bridge. This is the one thing about my job that hasn't become routine. The walk between the office and civilization is a pleasant reminder of why I spend half of my paycheck on rent. There's something enchanting about being close to the water. My mother felt it was important for her to be near water, but subscribed this need to her astrological sign, Cancer. I associate being close to water with freedom, the reminder that everything is in constant motion and if worse comes to worst you can drift away to somewhere better. Even when I lived in New Mexico with the relentless sun and the brown dryness of desert landscape, I focused on the foliage that managed to thrive, which resembled sea sponges and were perhaps relics that continued from the time, thousands of years ago, when that part of the world was covered by sea.

Is it possible to experience an event without tying it to one that has already happened? I can't think of a time when I visited a new place or met a new person without comparing the experience with another. This phenomenon is the main reason I return to work each day. It's not the worst job I've ever had.

The worst job was my first, when I was fourteen. At the time I was an aspiring actor and found there weren't many paying gigs where I could practice being in the moment and character immersion. A friend of mine, Emily, a tomboyish redhead who started smoking cigarettes when she was in the single digits, introduced me to her aunt. Mrs. Thompson owned the local party store. She wore sweatpants everyday and was quick to laugh, though her laugh always ended in a sickly coughing fit. I admired her fearlessness, but spoke quietly around her for fear that something I said would throw her into a laughing fit that would prove fatal. She hired me to attract customers by waving at passing cars and pedestrians while dressed in various costumes.

Most actors never dream of such range. I was Sesame Street's Ernie, Jason from the Power Rangers, Donatello of The Teenage Mutant Ninja Turtles, a ladybug, the Easter Bunny, an orange bear, Clifford the red dog, and Barney—apparently the most hated purple dinosaur in the world.

School had recently let out for the summer. The Northern Virginia heat was exacerbated inside the rubber and fur costumes. But it didn't get to me because I was living the life of a paid actor. Plus, Mrs. Thompson always had cups of water and homemade lemonade ready for me. Inside, the store looked like a celebration, balloons of every color, cards and signs written in capital letters and upbeat exclamations. Being upstairs, surrounded by racks of costumes, felt like being backstage.

Mrs. Thompson ordered the Barney costume months prior to my employment, but no one had rented it and each time she nominated it for the day's character I suggested another. Finally, she said, "Even great actors are faced with challenging roles sometimes." I was too naive to realize she had successfully played my ego against me, a lesson I still have yet to learn. With gusto I stepped into the purple costume and marched outside.

Before I even had time to sweat, a Trans Am halted in front of me. The driver, a middle-aged man wearing a short-sleeved business shirt and tie, flipped me off and called me a "motherfucker." That was the first time I had heard an adult outside of my family or not starring in a Hollywood action flick use that kind of language. I stepped back, still on the sidewalk, but I stopped waving. For a moment I thought he was going to get out of his car and try to kidnap me. The oncoming cars behind him honked their horns. He restarted the ignition and tore away. The noise kept up after he was gone and I soon discovered the cars were honking at me and many of those adult drivers were flipping me off and yelling profanities.

Was I doing something wrong? Was I not a convincing Barney? After a while I realized it probably wasn't my portrayal of the character, but something more sinister and out of my control. Why did these adults feel the need to take out their fury on a purple dinosaur? What was this character to them? I had suffered through the show a few times while babysitting, but I didn't understand where the rage was coming from. I considered going inside. Did the party store take the same approach as show business—any publicity, even bad publicity was good? Maybe this was the reaction they had been waiting for and my heroic stance in the heat, in a hated purple dinosaur outfit would help launch Mrs. Thompson's business into the realm of the rich and famous.

At one point a mother and toddler who had just left the neighboring McDonald's approached me. Learning from the earlier reactions, I was on edge, half expecting this to be some sort of ruse, where suddenly the toddler would spout a string of profanities and claw out Barney's mesh eyeholes.

"Hi, there, friends," I said in the happiest voice I could muster.

"Are you really Barney?" the toddler asked. She looked up at me with excitement in her big brown eyes and for that second everything seemed like it had a reason and was not merely a random series of absurd events.

"I sure am. What's your name?" I asked as I shook her hand, a fraction of the size of Barney's oven mitt.

I was energized after the exchange with the toddler and her mother. Despite the honking horns and shouting adults, I stood proudly and waved to all in front of the party store. In my mind they were honking and yelling in adoration, like I had already become a famous actor and they couldn't believe we were breathing the same air.

I heard them before I saw them. Barney's mesh eyeholes don't allow much in the way of peripheral vision. A pack of ten-year old boys armed with sticks charged toward me. One yelled, "Die, Barney, die!" Another called Barney, a "bastard." From a passing car I heard an adult voice egg them on, "Yeah, get him!"

My run was more like a manic waddle, but I moved as fast as I could within the layers of padding. I could hear a rock or something hard ricochet off the sidewalk behind me.

Before I reached the door, Mrs. Thompson opened it and stepped outside. I ran past her and hid behind the counter. She told the boys to get back and when they were gone she laughed so hard she couldn't talk. Her voice was a strained whisper when she said, "We were waiting to see how long you'd last out there," and then started up with the laughter all over again.

That was my last day at the party store, though not my last as an actor. I still wonder why those grown ups were so furious at the sight of a dinosaur called Barney, especially when the bigger problems of the world like poverty and war are ignored by a collective disease referred to as apathy. Maybe the simplicity of a children's character was easier for them to relate to. Or maybe the character was a rude reminder of the dreams they once had when they were young, the ideal of unconditional love that Barney sings about, before they discovered life was more complicated and out of their control.

On the way back from lunch, I imagined what I might say to the homeless woman. Should I explain to her that I didn't mean to be discourteous and explain that she reminds me of my mother? Why should I burden this poor woman who I've already insulted with stories about another troubled woman?

I saved half of my sandwich for her and returned to the park. This time I avoided eye contact, embarrassed by my earlier behavior. I held out the paper bag. She folded her arms. When I looked at her, I saw her face was smudged and contorted in anger. She hadn't asked for food or anything from me, unlike my mother. She just wanted to sit in the park, undisturbed.

"I'm sorry," I said.

I decided as I walked back to the office that the only way to stop being haunted was to stop connecting the past and present before the present has a chance to happen. Actors call this "being in the moment." Maybe this was the reason I spent most of my life trying to be an actor, to learn this one concept, the lantern to help me maneuver through the treacherous path of living. That I continue searching for reasons at all confirms that I haven't become a cynical adult, the kind that would berate a purple dinosaur. Of course this also means that I still haven't learned how to be in the moment and that searching for reasons is just a way to distract myself from a dead end job, a dead end life.

Back at the office, I pretended to be in the moment during a phone conversation with a client as Harry, the VP, passed my cubicle. This time I wouldn't run away. If he tried to interfere I would take a stand and defend myself, maybe even quit on the spot. This idea added a boisterous edge to my performance and for once he seemed to buy my act.

ACKNOWLEDGEMENTS

ABOUT THE MOTHER/DAUGHTER MONOLOGUES PROJECT:

Editor: Emily Cicchini, *Literary Manager,* **ICWP**, 2007-2009

Project Coordinator: Karin Williams

Reviewers: Alicia Grega, Anne Hamilton, Bethany Wood, Diane Wilder, Janet Bentley, Jules Odendahl-James, Lisa Brathwaite, Maria Beach, Melinda Finberg, Priscilla Page, Rima Dadenji, Roberta D'Alois, Talya Rubin, and Tami Canaday.

Special Thanks To: Margaret McSeveney, Paddy Gilliard-Bentley, Kristin Lazarian, Geralyn Horton, Meg Barker, Jenni Munday, Karen Jeynes, Kathy King, Annie Lower, Lillian Cauldwell, Lucia Verona, Lindsay Marie Jones, and all the members of **ICWP**—past and present—who made these books possible.

ABOUT THE INTERNATIONAL CENTRE FOR WOMEN PLAYWRIGHTS:

The International Centre for Women Playwrights (ICWP) is a non-profit membership organization with a mission to support women playwrights around the world. Since 1997, the group has operated continuously as a virtual centre, providing online networking opportunities, professional development grants, periodic writing retreats, and funding for public events and readings to raise awareness of women playwrights. The group is a 501 (c) 3 organization managed by a Board of Trustees elected by and from the membership. Membership is open to all people who support women playwrights.

http://www.womenplaywrights.org

*Proceeds from the sale of these books will assist **ICWP** to fulfill its mission by enabling more women's plays to be printed, promoted and produced across the world*